The Hanged Men

Novels by David Harper

HIJACKED
BIG SATURDAY
THE GREEN AIR
THE PATCHWORK MAN
THE HANGED MEN

The Hanged Men

DAVID HARPER

A NOVEL OF SUSPENSE

DODD, MEAD & COMPANY · NEW YORK

m   c.1

Library of Congress Cataloging in Publication Data

Harper, David.
    The hanged men.

    I. Title.
PZ4.H292Han [PS3558.A62477]   813'.5'4   76–25557
ISBN 0–396–07346–8
                          BL

This story is dedicated to FRED BOYSON
*who taught the author about the woods
and hunting the white-tailed deer.*

1

The hanged men dangled in ripe clusters from the starkly bare branches of the autumn trees. Looking down the snowy country road, I counted nine of them between our jeep and the next curve, two hundred yards north.

Their clothing was old, drab, ragged. They turned slowly in the breeze. Blazing red leaves sifted down gently and touched their shoulders.

Distantly, a dog howled.

"That makes nearly fifty we've seen since we left Old Forge," said Sam Keith.

"Fifty-three," I said.

In one smooth motion, Sam lifted his 12-gauge Remington shotgun and fired. The hanged man most distant from us jerked under the impact of the solid lead deer slug.

1

Sam laughed. "That's two hundred yards, easy. Let's see you match that, buddy."

"That was stupid, shooting down a road."

"Nobody's coming, and there's a hill at the curve."

The echoes of the shot were still rolling around the Adirondack hills. Tomorrow they would have been replied to by dozens of other distant shots. But today was the day before deer season opened, and the woods were still quiet.

So were the hanged men. The one Sam had shot still turned slowly on his twisted rope.

"Who puts them up?" I asked. I had been coming to the mountains for years to fish in the spring, but this was my first visit in the fall, and the first time I had ever seen the hanged men.

"Kids, mostly," said Sam. "They take old clothes, stuff them with straw."

"Why?"

"Who knows? They've been doing it every Halloween since I can remember." Sam lives in Old Forge, New York. He's got a shock of black hair that never seems to be tamed by the jugs of hair oil he combs through it. His eyebrows are bushy enough to harbor a covey of quail, and as black as ink. His mouth is broad, and usually holds a half smile. There is a rattle of gravel in his voice. We met one bloody afternoon in Paris when we were "volunteered" into an attempt to retake an El Al jet from five Arab terrorists. Nobody gave a damn for the jet plane, the Arabs, or the other hundred and ten passengers. But aboard was a particular under-secretary of state from Washington, and that made it our business.

Sam dropped two of the Arabs before taking the slug that permanently stiffened his left leg. I got the other three, but not before one managed to pull the pin on a grenade that blew up the flight deck and two crew members. One was a pretty dark-haired stewardess. I was unlucky enough to be the first one into the compartment, and she stared at me with stunned, frightened eyes while she died.

As a result of that action, Sam was retired from the unpublicized, unadmitted special forces squad of the C.I.A. As for me, I was forced to resign, under political fire, after I helped blow the whistle on a little caper known as Watergate. Now Sam lives in a small upstate New York town and runs a gun shop. Me, I sort of drift around. Solving problems. I'm not a private investigator. No way. If my fingerprints ever turned up on a P.I. application, the computer bells would ring so loud it'd sound like the 1812 Overture.

There's a guy you may have read about by the name of Travis McGee. He's a one-man salvage operation for people who have been screwed. He goes out and recaptures whatever they lost and takes a percentage. I enjoy reading about Trav, because in a sense he and I are in the same business. I salvage towns. On a strictly illegal basis, I hasten to add, because I am unlicensed, unauthorized, and usually unwelcome. In the old West, I might have been known as Wyatt Earp or Bill Hickok. Some have said I have the same rough exterior of those gentlemen. My hair is a sort of brown, and it is usually cut in a bristling crew style because I can't be bothered with flowing locks in my eyes when I'm busy trying to keep somebody from busting my head open. My nose is hawklike, and my eyes are a pale blue. I stand six-one and usually manage to keep down to my fighting weight of 185. Without boasting, had I gone into acting instead of my present line of work, I think I would have had a good shot at acing Charlton Heston out of the role of Ben Hur. At least, that's what a lovely drama student in New York once told me.

Anyway, as to my slightly shady way of making a living, when the dirty tricks plumber squads get out of hand, a few concerned citizens band together, put up enough cash to lure me out of my Kentucky cabin on the Rough River, and the next thing you know, newspaper headlines are reporting the suicide of a crooked mayor or the disappearance of a corrupt police chief.

Does that make it sound too easy? It's not. I learned long, long ago never to underestimate my opponents, a lesson that was reinforced dozens of times during my tour in the C.I.A. zap squad. Never turn your back on a nice old lady because as sure as God made little green grenades, she is going to roll one under your car while you concentrate on the harmless storm trooper across the street.

I have no idea what my life expectancy is in this line of work. The insurance companies haven't gotten around to establishing an actuary table on it.

"Warren," Sam said. "Look at that!"

I looked. A large buck, colored a rich glowing brown, had come out into the road. He stared at us, surprised to find intruders in his territory. His neck was swollen with rut.

"Eight points," I said, counting the tips of his horns.

"He's a beauty," Sam whispered. His hand touched the well-worn stock of his shotgun.

"No," I said, and gave a piercing whistle, the one that usually brings the woodchucks out of their holes when I'm out varmint hunting. The buck stiffened and then, in a graceful leap, he vanished.

"You didn't have to do that," Sam said. "I wouldn't have drawn down on him."

"And now you're not tempted to."

He uttered a few mild curses. "You're too good to be true. No wonder they threw you out of the Agency. Can't you abide anyone to have just one little weakness?"

"You always get your deer every year," I said. "Why louse it up by taking one the day before the season opens?"

"I've eaten August venison out of your pan," he accused.

"Taking a scrub animal for food's one thing. Stealing a good trophy like that buck is something else. Come on, Sam. Would you feel right putting his rack over your mantle, knowing how you came by him?"

"No," he admitted. "But I still don't need you to play conscience for me." He turned the key in the ignition. "Let's get on up the road. I want to check that herd north of the stream."

Anyone who hunts will be familiar with what we were doing. Driving around, scouting the deer herds, trying to locate the good bucks who, at this time of the year, are wandering around a fifty-mile circle, servicing every doe in their territory. By tonight, we'd have made up our minds where to be at the opening of season, dawn tomorrow.

Sam was still grumbling as the jeep creaked into motion. "I'll never see that buck again. They carry calendars in their heads. He knows just as well as we do that the season doesn't start until tomorrow. Come dawn, he'll be holed up ten miles down the stream."

We were approaching the curve where he'd shot the last hanged man.

I saw something from the corner of my eye, and touched his arm. "Hold it, Sam."

He stopped the jeep. I got out and went over and stood under the hanged man.

The hanged man was bleeding.

2

My full name is Warren Stone. No middle initial. I was born in Beaver Dam, Kentucky, on December 7, 1941 —just about the same time as the Japanese were bombing Pearl Harbor.

It was in those rocky hills that I grew up, hunting and trapping with my father and my uncles. The draft got me in 1962, and sent me to Germany as an ignorant private first class. Two years later, I returned to the States with staff sergeant's stripes on my arm and a light colonel's credentials in my wallet. I had gotten into Army C.I.D.—the Criminal Investigation Division— and what I lacked in education, I made up with hunter's instinct and toughness. Back in Kentucky the rules had been strict. You didn't call a man out unless you meant to put him down for good. If wronged, you didn't accuse a man unless you were so certain in your own mind that the subsequent trial and punishment were a matter of course. If you had a hunch that sharp trial tricks might get him off, you simply saw that he never made it to the courthouse.

The C.I.D. didn't officially endorse this attitude. But they didn't come down on me heavy, either—so long as I was right, and I always was. I don't know what they thought of me, but the promotions came along regularly, until I had the secret rank of lieutenant colonel.

After my discharge—actually, I never got a discharge, because I was shuttled right from the airport to a room in the Pentagon in Washington, D.C.—I was recruited by what I thought was a Presidential Security Team. It took me months to find out that it was actually a covert branch of the Central Intelligence Agency. I was never completely happy working for the Agency. For one thing, they lied a lot. Not only to the public, which I probably could have accepted, but also to those of us who were putting our tails on the line to carry out their orders. It was impossible not to notice that our enemies had a fuzzy way of changing. One month we would be busy as beavers keeping Generalissimo So-and-So in office. The next month, we'd be passing out grease guns to the underground so they could blow him away. Few assignments were as clear-cut in their issues as my Paris action against the terrorists. There, right and wrong were clearly defined. It all came to an end for me in 1972 when I found myself instructed to do a number on Armstrong, the Washington columnist. There was no way this could be in the national interests, not except in the warped heads of the forty men who made up the secret government, and who gave the C.I.A. their marching orders. I pulled in my horns and ran for cover. Recently, Armstrong was surprised to discover that he had been marked for execution. As Washington's toughest and most controversial columnist, inheriting the mantle of Drew Pearson, Armstrong had blown the whistle on everything from the CIA zap squad to Senator Eagelton's history of mental illness. I figure he owes me a drink, because I went right to Archibald Cox and spilled everything I knew, and that made it impossible to reassign the contract on Armstrong. I was Armstrong's hit man, and I wouldn't do it, and that marked the end of my career. When I gave my secret testimony, two Senators shook my hand and said that if there were more like me in Intelligence, we might not be behind the eight ball over the world. Funny. That was the last I ever saw of those Senators, and also the last I've ever seen of my back pay, pension, insurance, and all the other goodies we Americans have been educated to expect in return for good and faithful service.

Twice since then somebody has tried to kill me. Who is "somebody"? You make a guess.

So what does a cashiered zap squad man do to make an honest living once he's been put on the termination list?

Town taming is what I drifted into. I'm realistic enough to admit that there is a disturbing undercurrent of violence inside me. So, instead of being destructive, it finds acceptable outlet in cleaning up the messes otherwise responsible citizens have let their towns become.

But my presence today in Old Forge, New York, had nothing to do with business. Last year, Sam Keith had paid me a visit and we caught all the wall-eyed pike out of the big Rough River lake. He promised me a ten-point buck if I'd hunt with him next deer season in New York, so I agreed, and when November rolled around, I was between assignments. I drove up in my battered Dodge van, arrived early this morning, checked into a motel, called him around noon, and here we were with a hanged man dripping blood at our feet.

Deer hunting in New York State is divided into two tiers—Northern and Southern. In the north you can use a rifle, since the terrain is mountainous and will soak up stray high-powered rifle slugs. In the south a single shotgun lead slug is required. No buckshot allowed, as in the south. I had my sporterized Springfield '03, with a four-power Redfield scope. But Sam had insisted on using his Remington 12-gauge shotgun with the Quick-Point sight and solid slugs. "I'm going to be hunting down south next season," he said. "I want to get used to this Quick-Point."

I had to agree, it took some getting used to. Instead of cross hairs, you looked—with both eyes open—into the sight and saw, without magnification, your target with a bright red dot superimposed over it. It floated just above the gun's barrel, and the theory was that wherever you put that red dot, your slug hit.

Sam had just proven that theory by putting a half-ounce slug of lead into a Halloween hanged man two hundred yards away.

Except, instead of scattering brown straw to the wind, the Halloween joke was now leaking blood onto the fallen pine needles.

Sam shinnied up the tree and cut the hanged man down. The body made a dull, crunching sound on the frozen ground.

I bent over. The dead man's face was dark and congested, and his blackened tongue protruded.

"He was alive when they strung him up," I said. "He strangled."

His flesh was ice cold. But so was the air. I opened his jacket. It was new, as were the rest of his hunting outfit.

Sam's slug had taken him in the lower belly.

"The blood had pooled down there," I said. "It hadn't congealed yet, so that's why he bled. But he's been dead for hours."

Sam's face was white. "Thanks much," he said. He spat. I didn't blame him. My own mouth was watering too from barely subdued nausea.

"How much range has that CB radio of yours got?" I asked, nodding up toward the jeep.

"Maybe twenty miles."

"Put out a call. Get the state troopers up here. We'd better not move him."

"I'm going to have one hell of a time explaining that slug in his belly," Sam said. But he went over to the jeep

11

and, switching to Channel 9, started calling, "Emergency. Anyone copying this call, come on back. This is KWC-0867, Singing Sam, calling an emergency."

I heard the crackle of an answer, but couldn't make out the words. Apparently, with practice, Sam could. He said, "Move down to Channel Seven. This is Singing Sam, moving to seven." He switched channels on the little under-dashboard Citizen's Band transceiver.

The other voice came in clearer on that channel, and I heard it boom, "This is Mighty Mouth. What's your trouble, buddy?"

"Mighty Mouth, do you have a phone patch?"

"Negative. Who do you want to call?"

"State troopers."

"I'm dialing them. What's your message?"

"I'm on county road nine fourteen, six miles north of Old Forge. Got that?"

"Roger. The troopers are on the line now."

"Tell them we've got a . . ." Sam hesitated. I could sense his mind working. No point in laying it out for everybody in the county on the open airwaves. "We've got a serious injury. We need immediate assistance from the troopers."

"Roger," said Mighty Mouth, whoever he was. "Hold on." His voice became subdued as he relayed the message. In a moment, loud again, he asked, "The troopers want to know if you need an ambulance."

Sam hesitated. "No," he said finally. "No ambulance. That's a negative."

• • •

I caught a flick of the flashing blue lights before the squad cars came into view.

"Here come the troopers," I said. Sam looked up as the car came around the curve behind us.

He shook his head. "That's a black and white. County Sheriff."

The squad car coasted up behind the jeep. A big man with a handlebar mustache got out. He would have gone two-fifty easily. His nose, in the cold, was a bright pink. His movements were slow, but not one was wasted.

"How do, Sheriff," said Sam.

"Sam!" boomed the big man. "What's your trouble? I monitored some state Smoky transmissions. Seems they're on their way up here."

Sam indicated the body. "I took a shot at one of those hanged men. Only this one wasn't stuffed with straw."

The Sheriff bent over the crumpled figure. "You didn't kill him, though," he said. "This bird was already dead."

"That doesn't make me feel any better," Sam said. "Sheriff, this is my friend, Warren Stone."

The Sheriff wrapped my hand within his own. "Oscar Deep, glad to meet you. You live hereabouts?"

"I'm from Kentucky," I said. "Came up for deer season."

He studied me. "We've met," he said.

I shook my head. "No. I wouldn't forget you."

A whooping sound announced the arrival of the state troopers.

13

"Nice," said Sam. "That siren is scaring the deer over into the next county."

"City boys," said Sheriff Oscar Deep. "They think a buck is a dollar bill."

There were two of them, both very young, with ruddy faces and sharply creased uniforms. They were unhappy to find the Sheriff there ahead of them. They made up for it by giving Sam a hard time.

"It's against the law to shoot within fifty feet of a road," one said.

"It's also against the law to hang folks up in a tree," said Sheriff Deep. "Come on, boys. All Sam did was accidentally plug a corpse. Saved us the trouble of finding it next spring." Standing next to the troopers, both of whom went six feet, I now saw how big the Sheriff really was. He made them look like Boy Scouts.

One of the troopers searched the body. He found no wallet, no identification.

"We'll need a statement from you, Mr. Keith," said the other trooper.

"I'll see you get one," said the Sheriff. "My office will send it on to you."

"Sheriff—"

"This is a county squawk," said Deep, smiling without humor. "I was here first. You boys ought to learn these back roads, if you figure to enforce law on them. I'll do this for you, though. You can have the body."

The troopers gave up. Apparently they'd had experience with Oscar Deep in the past. One went back to the state car to radio for the meat wagon.

14

"I need a beer," said Deep. "Lenny's all right, Sam?"

"We'll meet you there," Sam said.

The Sheriff oozed himself into his car and scattered gravel and ice taking off. We followed at a safer pace.

"So that's your county Sheriff," I said.

Sam chuckled. "He's had the job since he was twenty-one."

"And he's now?"

"Fifty-seven."

"What did the county do, award him a lifetime contract?"

"They might just as well have. Every so often somebody decides to run against Oscar. He always loses."

"Is that good?"

"The voters think so."

"What do you think?"

Sam hesitated.

"Oscar worries me," he said.

He didn't have to say anything more. If Sam Keith had even the slightest concern about the big Sheriff, that was all I needed to know. Sam might not know precisely what it was about Oscar Deep that bothered him, but those hunches, if that's what you will call them, are precisely what kept agents such as Sam and me alive while other, smarter, agents were terminated.

Lenny's was your typical upper New York State roadhouse, a snow-strewn parking lot surrounding a low building with a huge chimney belching wood smoke that smelled deliciously of apple. Bright neon signs in

15

the windows hawked the wares of Utica Club and Genesee beer. Inside, the juke box held magnificent court at one end of the bar, its bright lights and swirling colors casting a flickering glare over the four men who were earnestly playing eight ball on the coin-operated pool table. A huge black Labrador dog sprawled, sleeping, across the entrance to the men's room.

Sheriff Oscar Deep was already there, and three bottles of Utica Club glistened on the bar.

"Cheers," said the Sheriff, lifting one of the bottles. It gurgled down his throat forever, until the bottle was empty. He sighed. "Good. First today." He slid the bottle to the back of the bar. I sipped at mine. It had a bitter taste that reminded me of the beer I'd enjoyed in England.

The bartender came over. "Another one, Oscar?"

The Sheriff shook his head. "Got two more hours on duty." He nodded toward us. "You know Sam Keith. And this is his buddy, Warren Stone, up from Kentucky. Came here to kill off all our deer."

The bartender, whom I assumed was Lenny, chuckled. "Welcome to them," he told me. "They're all over the roads. They had four good winters in a row, no winterkill, no dog packs chasing them down. We're up to our ears in deer. My wife hit one with the car last week."

"What's new about that?" asked the Sheriff. "I don't know anybody north of Binghamton who hasn't hit a deer."

"Yeah? Backing out of the garage?"

Deep laughed and Lenny moved away. The Sheriff turned back to us and said, "Sam, why don't you come down to my office later and dictate your statement?"

"You open until six?"

"Laura's there."

"Six, then. Warren and me, we're going to ride around some more. But after those sirens, we can forget about that upper road for sure."

The Sheriff chuckled. "Deer hunters. Nothing stops you boys, does it?"

"I'm not so sure about that," I said.

"What do you mean?" he asked, zipping up his heavy jacket and getting ready to go out into the cold again.

"That guy in the tree. Somebody sure stopped him."

Deep chuckled at that too. The Sheriff was a barrel of monkeys. To him, everything was funny.

Sam checked his watch. "Let's get moving, Warren. There's only a couple of hours of daylight left."

The Sheriff followed us to the door. "Don't forget to stop in and see Laura," he told Sam.

"Not to worry."

Deep had left his police radio on. It was squawking angrily. He gave us a casual wave, strolled over and picked up the hand microphone. "Deep here."

Sam and I had piled into the jeep. We heard the Sheriff communicating with someone who had an excited voice. When Sam turned the jeep key, the Sheriff got excited too, and yelled at us: "Hold it!"

Sam let the jeep motor wind down again. The Sheriff finished his conversation and came over.

17

"Big trouble," he said. He looked at Sam, then at me. "Maybe you boys better come down to Bear Paw with me after all."

"Why, Oscar?" asked Sam. "What's up?"

Deep ran the edge of one hamlike hand across his suddenly sweating brow. "Those kid state troopers, they got to thinking . . . if there was one body hanging from a tree, maybe there might be more."

The air was chill and quiet. I felt the old thrust of energy against my rib cage, my heart's get-ready-for-action response.

"Were there?" I asked.

He chuckled again, but this time it was a raw, angry sound. "So far they've found two more."

3

Laura Jackson, the Sheriff's secretary and—as I learned later—girl Friday, was slim, efficient and beautiful. Her hair was jet black, and so were her eyes. She had a broad smile, and her lips had that natural red that drives lipstick manufacturers insane. Her voice was a husky velvet. She nodded at Sam, accepted my introduction calmly, handed Oscar Deep a sheaf of papers. "Phone calls," she said. "You'd better start with the Mayor. Then Captain Porter over at the State Police barracks."

"I already talked with him on the radio," Deep said. "Gets rattled real easy, don't he?" He studied the slips of paper. "You boys excuse me for a couple of minutes, will you? But stick around. Sam, why don't you give Laura your statement? Then I want to talk to you about something else."

He went inside a small office, closing the door behind him.

Laura Jackson picked up her steno book, hesitated. "Sam, have you called your wife?"

"Jenny? Why?"

"Come off it. You know how fast stories carry up here. Use my extension. She's probably worried sick."

Sam shrugged. She handed him the phone. Then she and I went over to the Silex coffee maker and she poured me a cup of the darkest, vilest liquid I'd seen since I last drained my crankcase oil from the Dodge. The brew didn't let me down in the taste department, either. It sent my stomach scurrying for shelter.

Laura smiled. "They say you can't ruin drip coffee. Oscar is living proof that you can."

"The Sheriff made . . . this?"

"Surely you wouldn't accuse *me*."

"No," I said. "I guess not."

"I understand you and Sam are old friends."

"Like you said, news travels fast up here."

She tilted her head, laughed. "Oh, we may not have computer terminals tied in directly with the National Crime Commission, but in our small way, we keep on top of things."

"I think I heard something about that," I said.

"About our famous Syndicate convention, with all the overlords of organized crime?"

"I remember something in the newspapers. What— two, three years ago?"

"Three."

"Time flies."

"I was just out of college. It was my first year here in the office."

"What college?"

"Harvard. Graduate school."

She caught the look on my face.

"Do you find that odd, Mr. Stone?"

"No, I guess not."

"You'd assumed Vassar?"

Now it was my turn to laugh. "No, not Vassar. What took you to Harvard? Business Administration?"

"Law."

I suppose my eyes must have flicked around the dingy office. She caught the movement and hurried to say, "Only, I found after I graduated that unless I wanted to work down in New York City . . . which I didn't . . . that lady lawyers aren't in particular demand up here in the wild woods. I starved for a few months staring at my shingle, and then Oscar came to the rescue with a job that uses at least part of my potential, and here I am. Every now and then I draw up a land deal closing, and that helps pay my dues to the Bar Association. It keeps the wolf from the door."

"Not to mention bears?"

She smiled. Her teeth weren't perfect, but she had probably been using that erotic toothpaste they keep pushing on television. Her mouth had sex appeal.

"You mean, this town of Bear Paw? Actually, the town takes its name from that lake out there—which, if you'll look at a map or an aerial photo—resembles a giant bear's paw print."

"Another illusion gone. What about the Syndicate convention three years ago?"

She glanced over at Sam. He was busy talking into the phone. "The Sheriff got onto it first, him and one of his deputies. This is a small town, surrounded by a lot of wild country. It's hard for strangers to fade out of sight here. Oscar realized that a large number of people were gathering up at Judge Dassow's old mansion. It was a convention of land speculators, or so they said, but the Sheriff didn't buy that, so he did some checking."

"And he found out that the top gang leaders of every state had gotten together for a big powwow?"

"Right on. Well, it was too big for us, so we had to bring in the state, and the FBI showed up too. There was a big fuss, it made all the papers, but in the end nobody got arrested for anything serious. A couple of lapsed driver's licenses. One with nineteen parking tickets against him down in the city. Real big stuff."

"And meanwhile, the feds had been photographing every license tag in sight."

"So we heard. You know, those G-men aren't very co-operative with us local law folks. They take a lot, but they don't give much back."

"Yes," I said. "That sounds like the bunch I used to work for."

"Which you *and* Sam used to work for."

It was a statement, not a question. The lady had been

doing her homework. I nodded. "Guilty. We thought we were being heroes. We were wrong."

"Maybe not," she said thoughtfully. "All the results aren't in yet."

I heard a clang of abused phone bell as Sam hung up. He came over and poured himself a cup of the battery acid. "Women," he grumbled. "She's mad because you're not staying with us, Warren."

"She'd be madder if I were," I said. "I like to roam during the night."

He turned to Laura. "What does Oscar want with us?"

"Give me your statement, and then I'll ask."

So he told her what had happened up on the mountain, and she scribbled it down in some weird mixture between Gregg shorthand and Speedwriting.

"Finished," she said. "Sam, you ought to have your hunting license lifted. Shooting right down a road."

"Dirt road, nobody coming, hill at the end . . ."

"Still," she said. "If you hadn't shot—"

"What?"

"Those bodies might have hung up there all winter. Frozen. We wouldn't have found them until it got warm."

"Or, until the bears got hungry," I suggested.

"Funny, funny," she said.

"What about Oscar?" Sam persisted. "What else does he want?"

"What about me?" boomed the Sheriff, returning to the main office.

"What the hell else do you want out of us?" Sam demanded.

"Didn't I say?"

"Not a word."

"I want to put you boys to work. Sam, you know these back roads better than anyone I know in the county. I've already got my deputies on the move. But we need more help. Those troopers, once they get off the hardtop, they go in circles. We've got to check out every place those goddamned Halloween dummies might be. You know what we're looking for."

"Yeah," grumbled Sam Keith. "More hanged men."

We didn't find any more humans dangling from the trees. We cut down a couple of dozen straw men, and that was all.

Sam had produced a flask of ginger brandy. It deflected the cold nicely.

"I don't like this setup," he said.

"Me neither. Too pat."

"Are we being set up?"

I studied the question. "I don't know. There's no real evidence. Why us?"

We had often brainstormed like this when on missions for the Agency. Free associating, not thinking about what we said, or qualifying our responses. That could come later. What counted at first was to establish a direct link with the subconscious which, I have always believed, is fifty times smarter than the so-called civilized portion of our minds.

Sam said, "How could anyone know that I would shoot at that first one?"

"They couldn't. But if you hadn't shot, what do you want to bet that something else wouldn't have happened to draw our attention to it?"

"Why?"

"Somebody wanted those bodies found right now, not next spring."

"Then why hang them at all? Why not just toss them out on Route Twenty?"

"The hanging must be part of the act."

"A warning?"

"Maybe," I said. "But for who?"

"Punishment?"

"For what?"

"Might be revenge," he said.

"Same question. Why?"

He sighed. "You know what, Warren?"

"Yeah," I said. "Let's go to Lenny's and have a beer."

So we did.

The pool players were gone, and the juke box was silent. We sipped at our Utica Club, ate some Slim Jim sausages. I shared part of mine with the big black Labrador, who had come over. He placed his huge, dewlapped jaw on my knee and took the sausage gently from my fingers, his long, white teeth flirting gently with my thumb.

"How much does he weigh?" I asked Lenny.

The bartender shrugged. "How am I going to get him

up on a bathroom scale? Pick him up in my arms? Like hell."

"What's his name?"

"Shadow."

"He sleep in here at night?"

Lenny chuckled at the ancient joke he was about to spring. "Mister, he sleeps *any*place he wants to!"

Shadow licked my fingers. He made a little grumbling sound, a friendly noise that I have heard often from dogs I have loved. Shadow was one of the good ones. He could share my Slim Jims any time he wanted.

"Warren," said Sam, "Jenny said if I didn't bring you home for dinner, I shouldn't bother to come myself."

"Why's she so feisty?"

"I don't know. She's up to something. She said to make sure that you changed your shirt, and shaved."

"I see. Sam, she's trying to fix me up again."

"Like always. Look, I can call and—"

"No. It gives her pleasure. Why not?"

"She likes you, Warren."

"I know. I wish she'd let me convince her she's wasting her time. She knows I'm married already."

"Of course she does, but—"

He let it hang there. So did I. What was the point in flogging it around the painful track again? I had made my final decision long, long ago. Good or bad, I was committed to it.

But I had not become a monk. I had nothing against a pleasant evening, or even a weekend. So long as it was

26

clearly understood that nothing was ever going to come of it.

"What time?" I asked.

"Seven. Okay?"

"Sure. We'll hit my motel, get me fit to be seen. Is there anyplace around here where I can buy some wine?"

"Warren, you don't have to do that."

"I *like* to do that, Sam. Humor me."

So we detoured to find a package store, and I bought two bottles of Taylor's Lake Country Red, and then we drove over to the Indian Head Motel, where Sam squeezed his jeep between rows of newly arrived hunters' cars.

My room was at the end of the low building, and I unlocked the door while Sam gathered up our guns and brought them along. I didn't go in, though.

"What's wrong?"

He had come up on me silently.

"One of my indicators is gone. A string I left across the lock."

"Maybe the maid was here."

"No. She came in before you picked me up."

"Bad." He touched my rifle. "Want me to load up?"

I hesitated. With a lot full of parked cars, with two dozen hunters in the motel bar joyously quaffing their beer and planning the big hunt tomorrow morning, who would seriously be attempting an ambush just yards away?

"No," I said. "Just stand clear."

My key in the lock had already alerted anyone who might be inside. So I just turned the knob, standing well to one side, and pushed the door open.

Nothing happened. I snaked my hand inside and flicked on the light. A quick peek showed me that the room was apparently empty.

Sam and I went in fast. He checked the tiled bathroom while I ducked down to peer under the bed.

"Clear," he said.

"Same here."

"Did you leave any indicators?"

"Shaving mug. The handle should point to one o'clock."

"Oh-oh."

"Moved?"

"It's at three now."

"We've had visitors."

"Do you have anything here that you wouldn't want made public?"

"Are you kidding?" I went to the ventilator grate and examined its Phillips-head screws. My indicators, smudges of cigarette ash, were still in place.

"What did you stash in there?" Sam asked.

"The usual," I said. There wasn't any point in cluttering his conscience with full details. The "usual" included my .357 Magnum with the skeleton grip, and the other assorted sharp and explosive objects that were my stock in trade. I hadn't expected to find any employment for them on this vacation trip, but they were such an essential part of my existence that it had never occurred to me to leave them at home.

"How do you get that stuff on an airplane?" Sam asked.

It was a trick question. We both knew all too well how well the federal law enforcement had screwed the American public. In the guise of reducing aerial hijackings (I absolutely refuse to use the term "skyjacking" which was made up by MGM), metal detectors and personal searches had actually been set up to make it much harder to transport "contraband" materials interstate. Cutting down on hijackings has been only a side benefit. The real purpose Mr. Nixon had for ordering such procedures was to make more drug busts, to harass people "on the list" and to scoop up as many undetected violators of a hundred technical crimes as possible. Why? Because it's easy to catch some poor soul smuggling a case of Coors beer into the forbidden eastern zone than it is to rap down hard on organized crime, and one Coors arrest looms as high in the crime statistics as one arrest of a ten-time murderer. Look at the lists yourself.

I'm not against scooping up the mice along with the big rats, you understand. But let's be honest about it. Don't call it anti-hijacking. And don't let the rats get away while the small fry are caught in the machinery of computerized law enforcement. Let's face it. How many top bosses of organized crime subject their luggage to airport snooping?

Sam was waiting for an answer. I gave it to him. "Sam, we both know there's a dozen ways to fool those detectors, and the best way is never to go through them to begin with."

I didn't have to say any more. Both of us have lugged enough heavy artillery on board jet planes to start another war in the Mid-East.

Showered, shaved (with the aid of the recently disturbed mug), and clothed in a fresh plaid shirt and jeans, I reset some indicators and we took off in Sam's jeep.

"Whoever searched your room knew what he was doing," Sam observed as we followed the jeep's headlights over a rocky dirt road. This, he'd promised, was a short cut to Old Forge.

"It was a good search," I agreed. "He was too good not to have noticed those indicators. He burned them deliberately, to let me know he'd been there."

Glumly, Sam said, "That's what I thought, too."

"Some hunting trip. Do you think the Agency's put out another contract on me?"

"Who's left to do it? Between Watergate and the Rockefeller Commission, most of them have been swept right out into the Potomac."

"Yeah," I said. "But where was Rockefeller when I needed him?"

We drove in silence for a while. Once, I thought I caught a glare of bright yellow eyes. Then a shadowed hunk leaped across the road.

"Deer?" asked Sam, tapping the brake.

"Cow. The eyes were yellow, not white." There is a strange quality about the eyes of wild animals when

30

caught in the glare of headlights. They can be seen a hundred yards away, burning at you through the darkness. Those of wild deer are a cold white, while domestic animals tend toward the yellow. Maybe it has something to do with their diet.

Slowly, Sam said, "It might be something strictly local. Maybe somebody around here thinks you've got some reason, other than hunting, for your visit."

"Somebody like who? Sheriff Oscar Deep? Somehow, I just can't see him creeping around my room. If he wanted to check it out, he'd just kick down the door."

"State C.I.D.?"

"Why? I'm not on their rackets list."

"Your town taming? We've got a couple of burgs up here that aren't all they should be. Maybe Albany thinks you've taken an assignment."

"So?"

"The troopers don't like anyone muscling into their turf."

"I thought they were about as honest as you could get."

"Most of them are. They're a little gung ho on traffic quotas, but you can't buy them. Or scare them. Not, that is, unless you happen to be their supervisor."

"Oh. That way."

"That way. Why should it be any different for them? We all jump when the boss pulls the strings. Warren, the C.I.D.'s got men good enough to have pulled that search."

"Granted. But why burn my indicators to alert me?"

He fell silent. "Party pooper," he said.

We came over a hill and found ourselves at a stop sign at an intersection with a hardtop road.

"Route Twenty," Sam said. "In five more minutes, it's martini time."

Actually, it took six. But we'd gotten trapped for a mile behind a log truck weighed down with the bodies of a dozen giant trees.

I was looking forward to seeing Jenny Keith again. A tall, willowy redhead, she'd married Sam after he was retired out of the Agency and returned to Old Forge. Once, after a carelessly accepted third Bloody Mary, she had confided in me that Sam had been her child-hood sweetheart, and that she had cold-bloodedly set her sights on him and outwaited her competition, the Agency, until that cold mistress cast him aside.

"I caught him on the rebound," she told me, her dark blue eyes glistening, "and I'll see to it that he doesn't get a chance to bounce again."

They had no children. On another meeting, this one nonalcoholic, she confided, "My fault, not Sam's." This was the time they had come down to New York City to meet me on my return from a rough assignment in Europe. One of my last Agency assignments, carried out just weeks before I discovered how the Agency was using me to deceive the very people I thought I was defending. "I used to have this thing about horses, while I was killing time, waiting for Sam. Instead, I almost killed myself. I pushed poor Debbie for one rail she couldn't clear." She patted her flat stomach. "No babies, Warren. Not ever."

"Adoption?" I suggested.

"No, that's wrong for us. Besides, with Sam I've already got one big baby. That's enough for me."

It wasn't, and we both knew it, but you don't argue with a lady. Especially a tall, red-headed one with enough guts and temper to equip a regiment of the Scots Guard.

"Candles," Sam grumbled, as we finally overtook the log truck, passed it, and left it laboring behind us on the winding hill road.

"Candles?"

"Jenny thinks candles are seductive. Any time she gets romantic, I can count on finding the candles out for dinner."

"Sounds like a good system," I said.

"Tonight," he predicted, "we get a double serving of candles. You're on the wrong side of thirty, buddy. Jenny's going to light up the sky with candles, you can take my word for that."

"Good for her," I said. "I'm tired of looking at your ugly puss. Candlelight ought to help."

"You know, Warren, she's not going to rest until—"

"Sam," I said quietly. "Drop it."

He hunched down over the wheel. "Damn it, you can't waste your whole life—"

"Sam!"

"She's *dead*, Warren. You've got to admit it."

"No," I said. "I'll never admit to that."

4

My blind date turned out to be Laura Jackson, the Sheriff's pretty secretary.

"Small world," she said, smiling.

"You've met?" said Jenny Keith.

"You already know that we've met," I said, kissing Jenny's cheek. "Don't play games."

She laughed. "Guilty. When I heard about the hanged men, I called the Sheriff's office because I was worried about Sam. I found out you were both on your way there, and that's when I had the idea of asking Laura to join us."

Laura peered at me. "Disappointed?"

"Not at all. Pretty girls, good food and wine, plenty of candlelight. What better way to spend an evening?"

"How did you know we had candles?" demanded Jenny.

I nodded toward Sam. "Ask Old Bigmouth here."

Small talk is a necessary convention of civilization, so we observed its requirements during dinner. Sam and I told funny stories about some of the ridiculous things that had happened to us on assignments; Laura made light of her failure as a lawyer and jabbed feminist slogans at me, daring me to pick up on them; I didn't; Jenny played Super Housewife, as phony a role as I'd ever seen. And so we got through the meal and the coffee, and both bottles of the Lake Country Red.

"Brandy?" asked Sam.

"And cigars?" added Laura.

"Negative," I said. "The Surgeon General doesn't approve."

"I was speaking for myself."

"Lady," I told her, "you smoke a cigar, and you'll ride home alone."

She arched an eyebrow. "I had intended that anyway."

I didn't answer. I didn't have to. My wheels were back at the motel. It had obviously been set up that Laura would offer me a ride home after dinner.

We took our brandy into the living room and sat in comfortable chairs before the fireplace, which was crackling cheerfully. There, the conversation got down to business.

"The office got a report about that first hanged man," Laura said.

"The one I shot?" asked Sam.

"Yes. Not to worry. The coroner said he had been dead for several hours before you blazed away. Guess who he was."

"Tell us," I suggested.

"Arnie Lindstrom. A small-time mobster from Pittsburgh. They say he was an enforcer for the River Gang."

"What kind of action? Dope, bootleg cigarettes, gambling?"

"The same. But when I checked our records, I found that he was also one of those we swept up that Syndicate convention three years ago."

"How about that?" said Sam. "What do you suppose brought him back?"

"Deer hunting season?" I said.

Sam ignored me. "How did you get a make on him so fast?"

"Fingerprints," said Laura. "By now, they probably know who the other two were."

"Are the troopers handling this phase?" I asked.

"Yes."

"Can you find out who they were?"

"Probably."

I sighed. "Okay. *Will* you?"

She stared at me. "The report'll be on my desk in the morning. What's the hurry?"

"It might be important. Please, lawyer lady?"

Her lips tightened. "Warren, don't patronize me."

"Sorry. I always make jokes when I shouldn't. I take it back. Listen, Laura, you know the business Sam and I used to be in. Well, somebody searched my room this afternoon. I don't know how I'm involved in any of this, but I'd feel a lot better knowing all I can find out."

"All right," she said, her voice softening. "Sam, where's your phone?"

"In the bedroom."

Laura got up and left.

"Warren," Jenny began.

I held up my hands. "Say no more. Listen, I don't have my knives out for Miss Laura. I even like her."

Jenny sniffed. "You've got funny ways of showing it."

Sam said, "Knock it off, Jenny."

"Warren," she asked, "are you up here on a job?"

"No. Honest. All I want is a little venison for the old freezer."

"You've got plenty of venisons down in Kentucky."

"True. But we're in short supply on beautiful redheads."

She discarded the flattery. "Cut the blarney, Warren. I want a straight answer. Are you and Sam up to your old tricks?"

"Honey—" Sam began.

I cut him off. "No. Positively and honestly, N.O. That's what spooks me about finding myself right in the middle of somebody else's mess. Things are coming at me, things I don't know anything about, things I don't know how to guard against. Jenny, I never take chances when I don't have to. If I *am* tied in with this in any way, I want to know about it while I've still got some options left to play. But I give you my word, so far as I know, it's all just a lousy coincidence."

"All right," she said, accepting my answer. The firelight made one side of her face all pink and rosy. I like fireplaces. There is one in my cabin down on the Rough River, and I feed it with chunks of hickory and oak. The crackling of the wood knots somehow makes the place feel less empty and lonely.

Laura Jackson came back. "Two more bad boys," she said without preamble. "One from Indianapolis, one from New Orleans. Both with long records and strong ties to organized crime."

Sam whistled. "And all of them hanging from our trees."

"Yes," said Laura. "Very interesting." She turned to me. "Any ideas?"

"Gang war, maybe?"

"Why here? The nearest chunk of Syndicate action is way down in Utica. And they're bush league compared with these three characters."

I looked at Sam. "I still don't find any connection with us. It was just our rotten luck to be driving up that particular road."

Laura asked, "Did anybody know that you were going up that way?"

Sam shrugged. "Someone might have guessed. I always hunt that part of the state land. Every hunter around here knows that. We all have a pretty good idea of where everybody's going to be. That way we keep out of the line of fire."

"Is there any way this could be connected with your government work?"

I answered: "I don't see how. Granted, at times, the boys down in Washington don't seem to be playing with a full deck, but what would be their reason for stringing a trio of small-time thugs up in the apple trees?"

"Full circle," said Laura. "All right. Let's just drop it and wait to see what happens."

"Let's," said Jenny Keith, reaching for the bridge deck.

I am no good at playing bridge, so when Laura made the expected offer to drop me off at my motel on her way home, I had already gone down fifteen bucks and was glad to quit. Jenny was the big winner, with mostly my money in her pile. Laura and Sam came out just about even.

"Come again, victim," Jenny chuckled, leading us to the door.

"Fat chance," I said. "I know a hustle when I see one."

Sam said, "Sunrise—official sunrise, that is—is at six-thirty-two. I'll pick you up around five."

"Bring coffee."

"Buckets," he said. "Laura, thanks for dropping the big loser off. It saves me a round trip."

"My pleasure," she said.

Jenny brushed my lips with her own. "Have fun, big boy," she murmured.

"You," I whispered back, "have a dirty mind. For which, many thanks."

"Saddle up," said Laura, heading for her car—a dirty brown 1963 Chevy Impala. "Thanks for dinner, Jenny."

"Let's have lunch later in the week," Jenny called. "While all our men are huffing their way up the mountainsides."

"It's a deal." Laura got in, behind the wheel. I opened the other door and joined her. The car smelled like chocolate.

"What have you been doing with this heap?" I asked. "Trick or treating?"

"The candy smell?" She ground the starter. The Chevy grumbled through a few revolutions, then caught. "A friend of mine works for an outfit that makes food ingredients. He gave me fifty pounds of cocoa to take up to the hospital. One of the bags leaked."

I sniffed. "It's a good thing he didn't give you fifty pounds of ground garlic."

Laura drove well, concentrating on it. Once the Chevy got moving, it hugged the road and took the sharp curves without complaining.

Sensing my question, Laura said, "This Impala is the best mountain car Detroit ever made. It's got positive traction, so one wheel won't spin out on the ice. I've taken it up hills that stopped the boys with their four-wheel drive."

"Do you hunt?"

"Not any more."

She had let it rest there. I didn't.

"Environmentalist?"

"Realist. I don't enjoy killing. I'd rather let some Chicago meat packer do it for me, so I can buy my steaks wrapped in plastic. I don't really mind that the animals have to die to feed my guests, I just don't want to watch them bleed."

"Believe it or not, neither do I."

"Oh? Then why are you up here in your hairy wool shirt carrying your freshly oiled blunderbuss?"

"Survival."

"What survival? Surely you too can afford to pay the Chicago butchers to do your dirty work."

"I can't pay them to keep my reactions fast and my instincts sharp. Only constant honing can do that. Come on, Laura, you know what I used to do, and you know what I do now. So stop with the games."

"No games, Warren. I'm trying to find out who you really are. Not who you pretend to be. You make a big point of coming on like James Bond. But that's phony. You're too solid to wrap yourself in that kind of fantasy. Warren Stone, who *are* you?"

The question had come far too early in our relationship. It is one I rarely allow even myself to ask.

Before I had to answer it for her, I was rescued. It was a somewhat violent rescue.

A bullet had just crashed through the Chevy's windshield. It punched a little hole in the shatterproof glass. White cracks radiated out from it like a huge spider web.

"Rock?" Laura said, and I yelled, "Bullet! Get the hell down!"

I grabbed the wheel with my left hand as she ducked down under the dash. "Put your hand on the gas pedal," I shouted. "Floorboard it!"

She did, and I guided the speeding car with one hand while I kept my head as low as possible. We swerved from one side of the road to the other, but I managed to keep us from bouncing off the shoulder. "Have you got a gun?"

"Not here. Is someone shooting at us?"

"They were." The Chevy's rear wheels broke loose, and I had to sit up to get us out of the skid. "I think they're a long way behind us now."

No further shots came. She took control of the wheel again. I checked out the back window. I didn't see any headlights behind us.

"Goddamn it," she said. "My insurance doesn't cover windshields."

"Be grateful. I'm sure it doesn't cover holes in your head, either."

Defensively, she said, "Nobody was shooting at *me*, Mr. Stone!"

I tapped the bullet hole. "This thing is closer to your side than it is to mine."

"Maybe they thought you were driving."

"Maybe. On the other hand, lawyer lady, I don't happen to own a 1963 brown Impala. And since neither Sam nor I knew that you were coming to dinner, there's no way we could have tipped it off that I'd be hitching a ride with you. So who knew anything different?"

She didn't answer.

"Did you mention it to anyone down at the office?"

Softly, as the car slowed down, she said, "I didn't mention it to anyone. There's no way anybody could have known."

"Then maybe they were after you, lawyer lady."

It would have served her right had I left her with the gut-aching belief that somebody was gunning for her. But that was too mean, even for me. So, as we each sipped a drink at the motel bar, I said, "You're too ready to trust people, Laura. I can think of half a dozen ways they might have known I was in your car."

"How? I really didn't tell anyone."

"Did it occur to you that I might have been followed? Or there might be a bug on Sam's phone? Or yours? Or maybe even a little transmitter neatly hidden in his living room? That's just for openers, honey. The electronics age has complicated our lives beyond belief."

"This is awful," she said. She fumbled in her purse. "I'm going to call the Sheriff."

I put my hand over hers. "No. Not yet."

"But you're in danger."

"I don't think so."

"You just said it was you they'd shot at."

"No," I corrected. "What I said was they hadn't shot at *you*. I don't think they really shot at me, either. Unless we had gotten a lot friendlier on our first date than anyone had a right to expect, there was every reason for them to believe there would be space between us on that front seat. And that's where they put the bullet. Right down the middle."

"Closer to my side," she reminded sourly.

"Bad shooting," I said. "I could have put it right down the middle. They didn't want to hurt either of us. They wanted to warn me. Just like they warned me this afternoon by letting me know they'd been in my room."

She finished her drink, trembling. "But why?"

"If I knew that," I said, "I wouldn't be shaking nearly as bad as you are."

Outside, she glanced toward her car, then at me. I didn't need any more hint than that.

"Come on," I said, taking her arm and leading her to my room.

"I don't do this, you know," she said, sitting in the big chair near the TV set. "I just don't meet men one day and go to their room that night."

"Nobody said you did," I told her. I handed her a strong Scotch and water. Mine was even darker. The booze just didn't seem to have any taste tonight.

She choked on her drink and coughed a little. "Then what am I doing here? This is crazy."

"We're huddling together for warmth," I said. "Like the sheep in the high pasture when the wolves are howling."

"Mr. Stone," she said, "you have left me far behind."

"Forget it," I said. "Drink up."

"You're wasting your Scotch," she said seriously. "I never, but absolutely never pass out."

"And I never, but absolutely never practice necrophilia. Your fair white body is safe, Miss Jackson."

"Mizz," she said. At least, that's what it sounded like.

"What?"

"Ms. Pronounced Mizz."

"Yas'm," I said, in my best Georgia corn pone accent.

She stiffened. "You're called Mr. and there's no marital status known or implied by the term. Well, Miss and Mrs. are obsolete. Ms. is our answer to Mr."

"Fine," I said. "But might I ask exactly why do you want to conceal your marital status?"

"That status is our own private business."

"Wrong, Mizz. So long as your hubby is responsible for every tab you run up at the department store, society has the right to know whether or not you have such a meal ticket lurking in the background."

"The law today gives women equal credit ratings with men," she said.

"*If* they have earned them. Listen, so far as I'm concerned you can call yourself anything you want to. I had a hankering once to be called Sir Warren Stone. I announced that fact, just as you have announced your Ms. But guess what? Nobody would obey my orders. I'm still plain old Mr. I didn't invent the title, I inherited it. Just like you inherited yours."

"You're offensive," she said.

"Deliberately so. Listen, we've got real and serious problems to solve nowadays. Maybe separate but equal doesn't satisfy the Supreme Court, but it suits me fine. If you want your share of the authority, you've got to take your share of the responsibility. Full responsibility! No fair running home to Mr. Househusband and throwing up your hands when you find out he doesn't have the juice left any more to pull you *or* the world out of your self-created mess. End of everything. And, lady, guess what? Who the hell cares!"

She stared at me, eyes wide.

"My God," she whispered. "What set you off like that?"

"Maybe I'll tell you sometime," I choked. "Meanwhile, you'd better look the other way, because I think I'm going to be sick."

I staggered into the bathroom, and I was.

She had held my head and given me a damp towel. "I'm sorry," she said.

"No. It's me. I always get this way when people start shooting at me."

"You said they were only giving warning."

"I say lots of things. Most of them are wrong."

"Do you want me to go?"

I caught her wrist. "No," I said. "Please don't."

Bed.

"I don't do *this*, either," she told me.

Then she did.

•　　•　　•

White snow on the blank TV screen. A rushing sound from its speaker.

I got up, staggered over, and switched off the one-eyed monster.

Just then, Sam Keith pounded on the door. I checked my watch. It was a few minutes after five in the morning.

Before I let him in, I checked the bathroom.

Laura was gone, but she had left a message scrawled on the mirror in blazing red lipstick.

PHONE ME, she'd written. Then: DO YOU MAKE HOUSE CALLS?

5

Sam had a Thermos of coffee, and he poured some of it into two of the motel's plastic glasses. It was laced strongly with brandy.

He didn't make any wisecracks, but he didn't disguise the sniffs his ample nose gave to the lingering traces of Laura's Chanel No. 5. Just as well. I was sleepy and grumpy, and my fuse was short.

"I picked a nice runway for us to sit on," he said. "You might just have your deer by seven o'clock."

"And if I don't?"

"We're joining up with another party. First we'll road-hunt for a couple of hours, and then we'll put on a couple of drives up on the Dassow property. It's posted, but we've got Harry Dassow's okay. In fact, he'll be with us."

"Dassow? Isn't that the place the mob had their big convention?""

"The Dassow mansion. Yeah, but it's gone now. Burned down two winters ago. Harry is the Judge's grandson. He never rebuilt. And the fields all grew up. They make good deer cover now."

Outside, I heard car engines groaning in the cold, turning over reluctantly in the pre-dawn darkness. Sam looked at his watch. "We'd better go."

I slipped into my goose down-filled armless vest, pulled my red plaid hunting jacket over it. My pants were heavy green wool, insulated from my legs by cotton long johns. Instead of boots, I wore felt-lined shoe-packs. Much warmer than leather, I had learned the hard way in Alaska's interior.

My mittens had a flap cut out of the right-hand one to allow the exit of my trigger finger. Finally, I donned the flame-orange cap. Presto! The Compleat Hunter.

Sam had left the jeep motor running. It belched white clouds of steam into the flood-lit parking lot.

As we headed north into the graying sky, I told Sam, "Somebody took a shot at me last night."

"I know."

Surprised, I asked, "How?"

"Laura called the Sheriff after she dropped you off. He called me to be sure there wasn't any trouble over our way."

I must have slept sounder than I should after Laura and I had settled down for what I thought was the night. She had either used the motel phone without my hearing her, or else she'd slipped out much earlier than I had thought.

"Somebody's trying to chase me off," I said.

"That's what Oscar thinks too. But who? And why?"

"Good question." I patted the pockets of my heavy jacket. They bulged with 30.06 bullets, carrying 180-grain soft-points that would explode through meat and bone and drop a two-hundred-pound animal in his bloodied tracks. In this last freezing hour of the night, they were small comfort to me.

The CB radio crackled. Sam picked up the mike. "This is Singing Sam. Come on back."

More hash from the speaker. But Sam had the knack of turning static into words. He answered, "Roger, Deputy Dawg. We'll meet you at Lenny's at oh-nine hundred. I'm gone."

"What happened to your call letters?"

Sam laughed. "Screw the F.C.C. They're not up this early."

"No, but their tape recorders are."

One of the favorite tricks of the Federal Communications Commission is to put a long-play tape recorder on a particular channel and tape a whole day's traffic. Then some clerk, at $5.90 an hour, would listen, making notes. In the end, a few malefactors would be fined for using nickname "handles" instead of their legally assigned call letters and numbers. Such investigations keep the F.C.C. busy—far too busy, for instance, to investigate the regular and systematic theft of the public airwaves by the television networks and the big radio stations with their hundred-thousand-watt transmitters. Somehow it is all right to pollute the clear channels with advertisements for vaginal sprays and salves for piles. But it's a definite no-no for Sam Keith to call himself "Singing Sam" instead of KWC-0867.

Sam guessed what I had been thinking. "Remember that Russian trawler job?"

"When you put out the phony Mayday about one of their catch boats hitting a sunken wreck?"

"Right. We nabbed them inside the three-mile limit with an illegal catch, and best of all, they had to dump all their spy gear overboard before the Coast Guard showed up. That must have cost the Kremlin a couple of million roubles. But the F.C.C. cited me for the Mayday, tried to revoke my license—until they found out I didn't have one—and then laid a fine of five thousand dollars on me. The Agency paid it. Under protest."

"I'm surprised, after that, that they'd even let you have a CB license."

"They didn't. KWC-0867 is Jenny's call sign. But with CB, anyone in the family can use it. Still, she gets nasty letters every now and then."

"If they're that chicken, why don't you observe their stupid rules?"

"Where would be the fun in that?" he said, turning the jeep up a rutted dirt road.

Sitting on watch for deer is much like staking out a suspect on an assignment. You need an arc of visibility for yourself, concealment, and—lowest on the list— some attempt at finding comfort.

I found all three on a fallen tree trunk fifty feet above a well-traveled deer runway. My position was halfway up a steep ridge. Sam had gone all the way to the top, where he could see down into the other valley. I unfolded a little square of canvas and put it on the log to keep my behind dry. Plastic is more compact to carry, but has a nasty habit of sliding around just when you are trying hardest to remain still. I kicked out footrests in the damp humus of the forest floor. I was close enough to a standing tree to use it as a backrest. Carefully, I turned to see how much freedom of movement I had. It was enough to give me good coverage of the deer runway below.

Deer, like men, are basically lazy. They will find an easy path and use it unless frightened away by danger. That's why the largest number of deer are usually taken in the first hour of the season. They will have been blundering along in their usual paths, unaware that those have been marked by the hunter.

That isn't to say that they aren't wary. Deer always sense unusual activity in the woods. They see more cars on the roads. They sniff the angry scent of Man. But, until the shooting actually begins, they will—more often than not—continue to use the familiar runways.

Carefully, quietly, I loaded my rifle. The slugs would leave its muzzle at more than two thousand feet a second. They would smash home with an impact measured in tons.

I eased the bolt home, checked to be sure the safety was on, lifted the weapon to my shoulder, and peered through the scope. It was still so dark that, even with the thick post jutting up into the center of the field, I couldn't find the cross hairs.

My watch told me that it was still almost an hour to legal shooting. But I had already heard the distant boom of several shots, as some hunter came upon a sleeping animal, or even took a "sound shot," firing blindly at some noise—which, as often as not, would turn out to be one of his hunting buddies.

How like the hunting of men this was. More of our agents are damaged by their own team than ever get zapped by the enemy.

I inhaled several slow breaths, and let them out while saying the number "One." My pulse, which had climbed as I labored up the hill, slowed. I felt a quiet peacefulness descending over me like an invisible blanket. My eyes were alert, my reflexes were ready . . . yet my mind had seemed to step back a little way from my body, which was relaxed and resting.

Quietly, I stood above and behind myself, observing everything, ready to act in an instant. Yet I was at peace and undisturbed by anxiety or physical discomfort.

If something succeeds, I don't argue—I accept it. This little trick of meditation had been taught to me by a friend in Japan. It works, so I use it.

Calmly, I watched the fog drifting across the little stand of pines down the hill. It was like floating above the earth, observing swirls of white clouds obscuring the continents.

I took stock. Here I had only been in the mountains a single day, and my safe area had been invaded twice.

I'd better explain that. For instance, when I am driving, I establish boundaries. Several car lengths ahead, the same behind. No one alongside. I maintain those safe areas. They will either expand or contract, depending on speed. When someone ahead of me slows, I either pass or hang back. If somebody starts tailgating me, I get rid of him. I force him to pass. Or if he won't, I may stop dead in the road. I allow no car on my rear bumper. And I will never run alongside with someone moving at the same speed.

Result? I have never had a moving accident. No matter what happens, I always leave room to take action.

I run my life the same way. I am the center of the universe. Those I love are in the next closest circle. Other circles extend outward, until they reach reasonable limits. Those beyond the last circle do not exist, except to be manipulated or eliminated. Which depends on how deeply they have penetrated my defenses.

Now, in less than twenty-four hours, my inner circle had been breached. My room had been searched. A bullet had been fired, probably deliberately harmlessly, yet still fired into a car windshield only inches from my face.

I was forced to act. My mind, hovering above my body there in the fog-shrouded Adirondack forest, made that decision. My physical head nodded.

Somewhere, over the next mountain, a rifle fired rapidly. Five shots. And countless echoes.

I smiled, remembering the old guide's motto. "One shot, meat. Two shots, maybe meat. Three shots, no meat."

Some nervous hunter had emptied his rifle at a shadow, or at the sound of an animal crashing through the brush. I checked my watch. And he had done it thirty minutes before he was legally a harvester of wild game.

Some rules are made to be broken. Like the one about CB radio nicknames. Stupid. The only reason for spewing out a string of call letters that nobody can remember is merely so the F.C.C. will have an easier time of catching the one guy out of a thousand who is using the airwaves for something seriously wrong. Meanwhile, nine hundred and ninety-nine good guys have to go along with the rule, so that enforcement on the one wrongdoer will be easier for the feds. And, of course, he will always be the one who does *not* use call letters, so the rule is self-defeating.

But there are other rules which extend into moral areas. Such as blazing away at a handsome buck just a few minutes before the season opens. If that's your idea, why bother to hunt during season? Use a flashlight and jack your prey at midnight back in September, once the velvet is off his horns. Or shoot him from the road one October evening while he grazes in the cut cornfield. No one can effectively stop you. But if you intend to be a hunter, then *hunt.*

I like to think these are my beliefs. They were driven home just five minutes later when I heard a quiet rustle of leaves, a dull thud of hooves, and a giant buck came out of the pines. He stood dead in the center of the runway, peering back over his broad shoulder. A beauty, he would have dressed out at a hundred and seventy pounds easily. The light was now bright enough for me to see a high basket-shaped rack that had at least eight points, and probably ten. He would be a perfect trophy, if your tastes run that way, and plenty of good meat for the freezer, too.

But my watch told me that the season would not open for another nine minutes.

So I didn't even reach for my rifle.

Does this make me virtuous? I don't think so. I just didn't want that buck badly enough to be willing to feel bad about him afterwards.

Besides, right now he was evidencing strong interest in his back trail, and that interested *me.*

A stick snapped under a careless foot somewhere in the pines, and the buck literally vanished. One second he was there in the clearing, and the next he had disappeared in a sidewards leap so fast that it took only a blink of an eye.

I slipped the safety off my rifle and waited for whoever had spooked the deer.

He came out of the pines slowly, his own rifle at the ready. There was something *wrong* about him. He didn't look like a hunter. His clothes were pure city. It was still too dark to see his feet, but he wore a trench coat, and one simply does not go hunting in a brown trench coat, not unless you want to end up tied onto some careless hunter's car hood.

He made the mistake all animals—and most hunters —make. He looked ahead, he peered to the left and right, he twisted to check behind . . . but he never looked *up*. I learned this on the banks of the Rough River at the age of eleven, and several Iron Curtain agents are in their graves because they never did.

He was stalking something, and a little throbbing hunch in my head told me that it wasn't venison.

I lifted my Springfield to waist level, aimed at his chest. At this range, even firing from the hip, I couldn't miss.

Then, because he was too green to ever think of looking up the hill at me, I gave him a little whistle. The woodchuck kind.

He stiffened. The fog oozed over him.

His hands tightened on the rifle.

"Up here," I said softly. "Be careful, friend. Keep that thing pointed downrange."

"Warren Stone?"

"I figured you were looking for me."

"Put down your gun. Let's talk."

"Not a chance. What do you want? And who are you?"

"I'm not alone," he warned. "We want to talk, we

came here to talk. But if you won't talk, we have other ways."

"Talk about what?"

"Get out of it."

"Get out of what?"

"You know what. Listen, Stone, when we heard about those three soldiers hanging in the trees, and we found out that you were up here, we knew right away that you'd been brought in to take a hand. But we don't want a face-down with you. Those days are over. It makes too much heat."

"Mister," I said, "I am not involved with anything up here except deer hunting with a buddy. You can believe that. Now, just back on out of here, and pass that information along to your friends. I'm not looking for trouble, so get the hell off my back."

"We can make a deal," he said. "When you get back to the motel, take a look in that air conditioning vent in your room."

"Why?"

"Don't worry, we didn't touch your hardware. We only left a package. It's clean money, Stone. Laundered through Mexico, not a warm serial number in the batch. Take it and split. You'll be doing yourself a favor."

"Or?"

"If you don't care what happens to you, Stone, think about your wife. What will happen to her if you're not around to pay the bills?"

I almost shot him at that moment. And he realized

58

that he had gone too far. He began inching back toward the pines.

"Hold it, you son of a bitch," I said. "Get one thing straight. If you—or anybody else, and that means *any* body—go near her, you'll have about twenty seconds to wish you'd never been born."

His voice changed. "All right," he said loudly. "You're turning us down. I'll report what you said."

He had gotten calm too suddenly. I didn't need to hear the click of a rifle bolt to know that somebody else was down in the pines. I whipped the Springfield around, holding it low, pointed toward the "click," and fired.

Someone screamed. As I swung the barrel back toward the first man, he abandoned his own rifle and dove into the sheltering pines. I heard him bellow, "You crazy bastard! You're dead! We'll burn you by sunset!"

I answered him with a second shot fired deliberately high. It sent him on his way. I heard him crashing down the hill, and the cries of his buddy to come back to help. My first shot should have caught him in the foot or ankle, although I had fired very low. I didn't like the noises he made, thrashing around and moaning. "Come on back and get your buddy, stupid!" I yelled, ducking down behind my log. "I won't shoot you. But from now on, stay out of my road. The next time I'll aim where it counts."

I lay on my side and slid two more shells into the Springfield, but there wasn't another sound from down the hill.

Meanwhile, as the sun touched the tips of the mountain peaks, the woods around me opened up with what sounded like a small war.

Deer season had begun.

6

Sam was amazed.

"Twice? You shot twice—and didn't hit meat? I don't believe it."

"I hit meat all right," I said, going down the hill to gather up the abandoned rifle. It was a cheap 30–30, virtually worthless for deer hunting. I wondered what gun dealer had flimflammed the ignorant city thug.

Sam agreed. "It's pure crap. A Red Ryder BB gun is made better. Who does it belong to?"

I told him about the man who had come out of the pines, and the other one who had tried to draw down on me from within them. We went in and found a patch of torn ground, flecked with blood, where he had clawed in his pain.

Sam picked up a little chunk of white bone, red threads of flesh clinging to it.

"Looks like you aimed low."

"Five feet below his rifle click."

"He's going to have a pretty good limp from now on," Sam said with satisfaction. He scowled at the bit of bone. "Any reason for us to keep this?"

"Not for me. I don't intend to file any complaint, and I doubt that they will."

Of course, even an expert can be wrong.

He tossed the bone fragment out into the pines. "Lunch for the foxes. Come on, pal, let's get the hell out of here. Those boys might come back with their big brother."

Lenny served up an Irish coffee that drove the chill out along with the snakes and anything else that might have been left over after Saint Patrick cashed in his chips. Even Shadow, the big black retriever, snuck away from its aroma.

Sam can do a good Jackie Gleason imitation. He did it now. "WOW!"

"Have any luck?" asked Lenny.

Sam indicated me. "Peanut brain, here, saw a ten-point nine minutes before sunrise. He let him go."

To my surprise, Lenny stuck out his hand. "Good for you," he roared. "I knew you weren't one of those god-damned road hunters."

"Don't knock road hunting," Sam protested. "I've shot more bucks from the road than anywhere else."

"You know what I meant," Lenny said, serving up two more hefty mugs of coffee and Irish whisky, topped with an Everest of whipped cream. "It's not just hunting from the road. Those bastards don't have any pride. They'll shoot anything that moves—buck, doe, fawn. Listen, last season, I had three of them in here. They were really pouring down the ginger brandy. 'We got one,' their big guy bragged. Well, we had a trooper in here, just getting a cup of coffee."

"WOW!" Sam repeated.

"*Real* coffee. You couldn't make a trooper take a drink on duty if you held a gun on him. Well, the trooper said, 'Terrific. How many points?' and the big guy said, 'Two.' "

"Two?" I said.

"Two," Lenny repeated. "The trooper figured something was wrong, he gave me a nod, and I switched on the outside lights. Those road hunters, they still didn't know what was up, and the big guy said, 'You know, I never saw a jet black deer before.' That did it. The trooper went out and checked. Sure enough, they had the critter tied up on top of their station wagon . . . tagged all legal. Except it wasn't a deer, it was some farmer's Black Angus bull!"

"Lenny," said Sam, "I've heard that Black Angus story every deer season since I got my first license."

"It really happened!" Lenny protested.

"Do you hunt?" I asked him.

"Sure. Follow me."

He led us out the back door.

Hanging from a tree branch near the barn was a huge nine-point.

Sam swore. "Lenny, you son of a bitch, you jacked that deer last week and stashed it in the freezer so you could hang it up this morning."

"Like hell," said Lenny, undisturbed. "See?"

He indicated the red, gaping body cavity, where he had dressed the animal out. It was steaming in the cold wind.

"How the hell do you do it, Lenny?" asked Sam. To me, he added, "He goes out the first hour of the first day, every year, and by coffee time he's home with a buck." He gave Lenny a gentle punch on the arm. "You salt down a tree stump, right?"

"You know better than that. I watch up that hill all year long. It gets so I start thinking like a deer. I own the whole mountain, you know, so nobody goes up there to spook the herd. I look them all over real good, and opening morning I collect the one I want before the guns start going off all over the county. And that's all I take, one, and I use him for my big venison dinner on Thanksgiving. To which," he added, "you and your wives are all invited."

"Jenny and I'll be here," Sam said, grinning. "I knew I'd needle you out of another invitation."

"Warren, how about you?"

"My wife's down in Kentucky," I said. "But I'll try to make it."

"Well, fine," he said. "Maybe she can come next year."

Sam started to say something, but I stopped him. "I hope she can," I said. "She'd like that."

7

Harry Dassow was a tall man, very skinny, with a shock of pure white hair. His face had no lines, and it was a healthy pink. He could have been anywhere from thirty to seventy years old. He moved more like thirty.

His hand was firm on mine. "Welcome," he said. "Sam's friends are my friends."

"Any luck?" Sam said. He waved for some more coffee. Lenny nodded and began pouring it.

Harry Dassow shook his head. "Lots of deer, but no horns."

I had been looking out the window when he drove up in a high-sprung Land Rover. It sat triumphantly in the parking lot, with its spare gas cans, like something left over from Rommel's Desert Korps.

Harry Dassow made an introduction. "Ben Shaw," he said, indicating a heavy-set man of perhaps fifty. Shaw had a shiny scar down one side of his face, and a cigar clamped in his jaw. "Ben's one of our lawmen."

"Deputy Dawg," Sam said, flicking an imaginary microphone switch. "Ten four."

"And on the side," said Shaw. He blinked at me. "You modulate the airwaves, Warren?"

"Not lately. Are you one of Oscar Deep's men?"

"Smile when you say that."

"No offense. I'm just looking for someone to report an incident to."

"What kind?"

"Two men came up on me in the woods and drew down on me with their pieces. I got in the first shot and chased them off."

His friendly smile had vanished. "Anybody hurt?"

"Not that I know of," I lied. "I fired wide."

"What did they want?"

"Search me. Maybe robbery?"

Sam was getting itchy. "Warren," he said, "we'll file a report over in Bear Paw. Ben here, he's not on the county force now, not this county anyway."

Lenny shoved the Irish coffees over the bar. "Here," he said. "Less talk, more drinking."

The third member of Dassow's party stepped forward. I hadn't paid much attention, but it was suddenly obvious that the small, quiet person in the green hunting jacket was anything but masculine.

"Thanks," she said. "My butt is freezing."

Her name was Joan Hartman, she volunteered that she lived in Montana, this was her first trip east, she was visiting friends in Deer Creek, where she'd met Harry Dassow, who invited her on the hunt.

She touched the orange license tag pinned to the back of her green coat. "Phony," she said. "I never shot anything in my life."

Her hair was that frosty kind of salt and pepper that looks like it had to come out of a bottle, so it was probably real. It still looked good. Her mouth was broad, and built for smiling, with a rosy lip glow that might have come from Revlon, or from the nippy cold outside. Again, who cared? I would have guessed her age as twenty-five, give or take a year. Her hunting outfit was obviously borrowed—everything was too big—but she fitted into it nicely. Like the man who writes songs said, cute as a button.

"You're staring," Sam told me.

"I guess I am."

"Busy little man. What about Laura?"

That pulled me up. Yeah, what *about* Laura? Had I told her last night where we would be hunting this morning? No, I couldn't have, because I didn't know myself.

Well, somebody had known.

"What's the schedule?" asked Harry Dassow.

Sam sipped his Irish coffee. Shadow, the big dog, came over and lay down on his booted foot. "I thought Warren and me'd drive around and road-hunt for an hour or so. Then we can meet up at the mansion and drive that side hill. We've got enough men. Put Warren and Joan on watch near the stone fence. You and me and Ben, we'll come up through the apple trees. I checked them out a couple of days ago. Those deer have left track all over that side hill, eating those fermented apples."

"Is that fair?" asked Joan Hartman.

"Is what fair?" Ben Shaw said.

"Driving the deer like the three of you were a dog pack? Out west, the hunters stalk them one on one. No dogs allowed, and no human dogs either."

"We're not out west," he said. "That's the way we've always hunted here. What's the difference between three of us deciding to go through the apples together on purpose, or three others going through at the same time by accident?"

"The difference is that it's wrong to organize the hunt like a military action," she said. "I'm really surprised that you don't use two-way radios to direct your attack."

Sam smiled tightly. Because she had hit close to the truth. He had mentioned to me earlier that he and his hunting pals were thinking of buying some walkie-talkies for just that purpose.

"I thought you said you didn't know how to hunt," I said.

She smiled at me. "What I said was that I hadn't *shot* anything."

"Oh? And how do you hunt without shooting?"

She returned my stare. "Ever hear of cameras?"

Ben Shaw cleared his throat. For a moment, I thought he was going to spit on the floor. "You can't eat color slides," he said. "Are we going to get this hunt on the road or not?"

Sam checked his watch. "Warren and I are going to drive around for a while. We'll monitor Channel Six on the hour and half hour."

"Hah!" said Joan Hartman.

Sam colored. "Maybe you'd like to trade in your rifle on a Kodak."

"No," she told him calmly. "It's time I shot something. Everybody keeps telling me what a big kick it is. I want to find out for myself."

I studied her. She was aware of my scrutiny, and her cheeks flushed slightly.

Harry Dassow put down his empty coffee cup, threw a five out on the bar. "My treat. Everybody ready?"

"Ready," said Joan, her eyes still locked with mine.

They left. Sam looked after her, and gave his Jackie Gleason "WOW!"

"That is a woman," Lenny agreed. "Except we might as well face it, Sam. She didn't have any eyes for you or me."

"No," said Sam. "That's what comes of letting a swordsman like Warren hang around. He skims off all the good stuff."

"Let's hunt," I said.

Sam drained his cup. I pushed mine away. I'd had enough coffee, Irish or otherwise.

The phone rang as we started for the door, and Lenny answered it.

"Hey," he called. "Come on back, Warren. It's for you."

I took the receiver. "Hello?"

Jenny Keith said, "I'm glad I caught you, Warren. Your father-in-law called. He said it's very important."

"Okay," I said.

"Do you have the number?"

"I've got it." Even in my own ears, my voice sounded cold and distant.

"Dear," she said. "I hope this isn't bad . . . I mean—"

"Thanks for finding me. Do you want to speak with Sam?"

She hesitated. "No, you'd better make your call. Just tell him to keep his feet dry." I heard her breath catch, and she almost said something else, but then she didn't, and I heard her hang up.

"I've got to make a long distance call," I told Lenny. "I'll charge it to my credit card."

"Be my guest." Politely, he and Sam moved away, down to the end of the bar. I gave the operator the number, my card identification, and Howard Pyle picked up on the second ring.

"Warren?"

"Yes. What's up?"

"I had a call from Louisville. Dr. Ewbank. He says

Alice's account is two months in arrears."

I swore, and he misunderstood. "Warren, I did my best. I offered him all we've got in the bank, six hundred or so. He said not to bother, that what we had wouldn't help much. He wants you to call him. Right away."

I thought for a moment. "No," I said. "I'll wait until I can see him face to face. Look, drive over to my cabin. You know where the key is. You'll find a metal box under the fireplace hearth. There's a loose brick. There's four, maybe five thousand in the box. Take it up and get things fixed up for now. Tell Doc Ewbank I'll have some more money transferred in a day or two."

"You aren't going to call him?"

"I'm going to call somebody else," I said grimly. Then, after a moment: "How is she otherwise?"

He didn't answer at once. "The same," he said flatly. "No change."

I hadn't expected any. "Thanks," I said. "I'm sorry there was this mix-up. Somebody goofed."

Hesitantly, he said, "Dr. Ewbank was very cordial. He suggested the state hospital again."

"No."

"You'd save a couple of thousand every month and the care is the same—"

"Howard, drop it. The care isn't the same, and we both know it."

"All right. But it's still good care, and she wouldn't know—"

I let him hang for what seemed a full minute while

I choked on my own bile. Then I said, "How do you know she wouldn't?"

He didn't answer. I hung up.

I had the operator get me the next number, in Carson, West Virginia.

The man who answered was grumpy, half-asleep.

"Mayor Borkh?"

"Yeah. Who is this?"

"Warren Stone."

A pause. "Oh, yeah. Listen, Stone—"

"No, Borkh. You listen. You promised to pay me twenty thousand dollars for cleaning up that mess in your town. You were supposed to deposit that amount to the account of Alice Pyle Stone in the Louisville Polytechnic Hospital. Why didn't you?"

"I had some trouble with the city council, Stone," he said, coming awake. "I thought they'd back me up, but—"

"So the fee you agreed to is now a subject of further negotiation?"

"Well, not so much that. I think you may have to adjust it downward. I mean, my God, we can't tell them what you *really* did. We'd all go to jail."

"Borkh, did you ever read the Pied Piper of Hamelin?"

"Listen, Stone, it's too early in the morning to—"

"He drove out the rats, remember? And the good burghers of Hamelin reneged on his bill, too. Do you remember what happened to Hamelin, Mayor?"

72

"Don't you threaten me, Stone. Your hands aren't clean."

"I never threaten. I'm telling you something, just this once. That money had better be transferred, by wire, this very day, because when I call the hospital this evening, if it isn't there, I'm coming back to your little coal bin, and this time I'll sweep out all the dirt, right up to the top. Do you get my meaning?"

His voice trembled. "I don't know if I can pry all that money loose. We've had a recession down here, you know."

"Isn't that tough? You've got until five P.M., Mayor."

"I'll try, but—"

"Try hard. If you need any extra encouragement, you might take a look in that little strongbox you keep buried under your back porch."

I heard him suck in his breath. "Why, you bastard—"

I cut him off. "Remember those postdated deeds of trust on the interstate highway bypass land?"

"You thief!"

"They're still there," I said softly. "But they've been photocopied. And there's a corner missing off each of them to authenticate my copies."

"Do you know how little a hit costs, you back-stabbing son of a—"

"On me? Borkh, your whole damned town couldn't afford it. Now, pay what you owe me and let it drop." I waited. "Borkh?"

"Ahhh . . ." The words choked him, but he said them.

73

"All right. You'll get your money."

"Thank you, Mr. Mayor," I said. "It's been nice doing business with you."

Road-hunting isn't my idea of sport. You ride around, keep your eyes peeled for any movement, for an odd shape under the trees. The tools of your trade are a four-wheel-drive vehicle, high-powered binoculars, and equally high-powered rifles with telescopic sights. You talk quietly as you drive—of other hunts, of other trophies, of casual things that aren't very important. You never talk of your fears or your failures.

"Warren," Sam said quietly, "look up by that tall pine. Glass the field."

I lifted the wide-angle ten-power binoculars, swept them across the upper edges of the meadow.

"Three—no, four," I said. "But no horns. All does."

He looked through the binoculars himself. "There's a buck up there somewhere."

"Probably back in the trees." It's a quiet joke among hunters that the white-tailed buck knows how to treat his lady friends. He sends them out into the fields first, to see if there's any danger. Only then does he come out to graze.

Sam handed me the glasses, and put the jeep in gear.

As we bounced up the dirt road, he broke the road-hunting rule.

"Sorry, but I couldn't help overhearing back there in Lenny's. How the hell do you afford it? Full-time care in the intensive care wing?"

"I afford it," I said.

"By putting your ass on the block every day and twice on Sunday. You can't keep lucking out, buddy. One of these days you'll cut it too fine, and they'll either pick up the pieces in a plastic bag, or else throw you behind bars."

"Sam, lay off."

"Why the hell won't you listen to the doctors? They keep telling you—"

I pulled the jeep key out of the ignition and tossed it down on the floor. Sam swore and threw the vehicle into neutral, coasted to a stop. "Warren, what the hell—"

"Sam, keep your goddamned mouth off me! I've had it with all of you, whipsawing me in every direction, all the time assuring me it's for my own good, that you're only speaking out of friendship. Well, stop it. For God's sake, Sam, don't you realize that I *wish* she were dead? I wish it a dozen times a day, and a dozen times a day I hate my own guts. I didn't volunteer for this, but I'm stuck with it, so stay the hell out of my business. Or say good-bye."

He picked up the keys.

"Okay, Warren. I'm sorry."

Slowly, I answered, "So am I."

We reached the ruins of the Dassow mansion early. We had missed radio contact on the hour with "Deputy Dawg" Ben Shaw, probably because of intervening mountain ridges.

The road up to the ruins was still in good shape, although half-blocked in some spots by snowdrifts.

"Who was Judge Dassow?" I asked.

"He used to own damned near all of the county. He was in logging, mostly. When they started forming the Adirdondack forest preserve, he had already made his pile, so he got behind the 'forever green' policy and helped get it going."

Dryly, I said, "Thereby keeping everybody else from making a buck too."

"That's the way it goes," Sam agreed. "They get old and scared of death, so they start buying Brownie points from God. Once they've had their first heart attack, they become very public-spirited."

I grinned at him. "Is this the Sam Keith we all know and love? How cynical you've become."

"I've had practice," he said.

We drove around the last bend and saw the ruins of the big house. The stone walls still stood, crumbled in the middle of one long expanse of masonry. It had been some joint. On the side facing us, I counted nineteen broken windows, staring at us like the empty eye sockets in a skull.

"And this is the site of the famous gangland convention?" I asked.

"The same."

"Why here? Was the Judge mixed up in the rackets?"

"Oh, he was long dead by then. Harry Dassow rented them the place. He claims he was tricked by the real estate firm who set up the deal. The authorities checked him out, and he came up clean."

"What does he do for a living?"

"He's semi-retired. He used to be down in Wall Street. Now I understand he fools around with futures —grain, potatoes. That kind of fast-in, fast-out stuff."

"A man can go broke that way. Maybe he's living off the Judge's estate."

"Wrong. The Judge died broke, except for the mansion, which was frankly a white elephant. These days, you couldn't hire—or be able to afford even if you could find them—enough help to run the place. Best thing that ever happened to Harry was having it burn down."

"I wonder if the insurance company feels the same way."

"Harry didn't carry any. There wasn't any mortgage, so he preferred to be self-insured."

Looking at the smoke-blackened walls, I said, "And he lost."

"At least his taxes went down."

Changing direction, I asked, "Who's this Ben Shaw? You got real up-tight about him back there in Lenny's."

"He's touchy," said Sam. "He used to be Oscar Deep's best deputy until a couple of years ago. Then, suddenly, Deep fired him. No reason."

"Couldn't Shaw have asked for a review?"

"Sure. But he didn't. He just crossed over to Hamilton County, got a job there on the force. But there's no love lost between him and Deep."

"What's he doing over here?"

"He's still got lots of friends around this county, one

of them being Harry Dassow. Harry's got him moon-lighting as a guard."

"Guard? Against what?"

"Vandals."

"The house is gone. What's left to guard?"

"Timber. This mountain has one of the last remaining stands of hardwoods big enough to be worth real money. The furniture manufacturers lick their lips every time they fly over. With selective cutting, not hurting the forest at all, Harry could take out the best trees and clean up a million bucks in a single season."

"Why doesn't he?"

"Ask him. Maybe he's waiting for the price to go even higher. There's a real shortage of fine wood, and it's getting tighter. Meanwhile, during the fall, when it's dry, he's a nervous wreck about wildfire. He closes this place off tight."

"Isn't this part of the Adirondack preserve? How can he timber it off?"

Sam chuckled. "The Judge got holy, but not *that* holy. He held back the timber rights on this section when he signed the rest over to the preserve."

"Sly old coot," I said.

A horn beeped over the hill. A moment later, Dassow's Land Rover charged up the slick hill.

Tied on its hood was a very large, very dead brown deer. It was a six-point buck, eyes half-open—staring glazedly at an unseen world. The tongue lolled from a lax mouth.

To Harry Dassow, Sam said, "See you got one."

"Not me. Ben spotted him up the side of Sawmill Mountain. Sat down right in the middle of the state highway and squeezed off. Dropped him with one shot."

Joan Hartman, examining the orange tag tied to the buck's ear, said, "Unbelievable. I never turned my head for a moment, but it appears that during the blink of an eye, Clarice Shaw shot this deer and then disappeared back down the mountain, leaving her husband to dress it out and put her tag on its ear."

"Everybody does that," Shaw said. "Cut it out. Clarice paid for her tag. This is her deer."

"Wouldn't it have been a hell of a lot more sporting if she'd shot it herself?"

"Easy, easy," said Harry Dassow. "Joan, the hard fact is that what Ben did, everybody else in these woods does too. We aren't trophy-hunting, we're meat-hunting. You'd be surprised at how many wives shoot their deer on opening day."

"I'd be surprised?" she said. "Not really."

His voice hardened. "You're not really having that much fun, Joan. Shall I drive you back to Deer Creek?"

"No," she answered, her voice just a shade too brittle and high. She was on the ragged edge of something. "Warren and I are going to sit up here on watch, isn't that right?"

"If you want to," I said.

She nodded vigorously. "I want to."

Dassow looked anything but happy. "Okay. Stone, you take the high end of the wall."

79

"What about me?" Joan Hartman asked.

"Sit anyplace you feel comfortable," he said shortly, turning toward the Land Rover. "Let's go."

Shaw and Sam piled in, and they drove down the hill. I walked over to the crumbling stone wall. It commanded a fine view of the sloping hillside.

"You and your boy friend seem to be striking a few sparks," I said.

Joan snorted. "He's no boy friend of mine." I raised an eyebrow, and she added, "We only met a few days ago. He's not bad-looking, he's not uncultured, he seems to have money, and—most of all, he's single. We went out a couple of times, and he invited me on this hunt."

"I think he just *un*invited you, too."

She laughed. It was a hearty, happy sound. "Did he ever! But I never did learn how to take a hint."

"Where in Montana do they raise ladies like you?"

"Ever hear of Cut Bank?"

"Never."

"It's right outside the Blackfeet Reservation, up near the Canadian border."

"Nice country?"

She laughed again. "If it were nice, would the Great White Father have given it to the Indians? It's a place of howling blizzard all winter and burning dust all summer. But I love it."

"When are you going back?"

She hesitated. "When—when I've finished something important here."

"I take it, then, that your visit to Deer Creek isn't merely pleasure."

Her third laugh was harsh. "Hardly. And that is your last question, Mr. Stone. Hadn't we better get into our positions?"

I examined her rifle. It was a brand-new .308 Winchester, with a clip feed. A four-power Weaver scope was mounted on top. I looked through it. The cross hairs snapped into focus against the distant trees.

"Have you fired this baby?"

"Of course. I know better than to go into the field with a strange rifle. It's sighted in exactly at a hundred yards. At fifty, it will shoot about an inch and a half low."

She knew her weapons. I tossed the rifle back to her. She caught it easily. I pointed to a little grove of spruce. "If you sit in there, you'll have a good field of fire over most of the hill."

"Where will you be?"

"Up at the head of the wall."

"What's your territory?"

I smiled at her. "Honey, if you see horns, blaze away. Don't worry about poaching on my preserve."

Her lips tightened. "All right." She wasn't sure if I were putting her down or not. "You asked for it."

She went down to the spruce grove, keeping her rifle pointed up at the sky. Good girl.

My own watch position was comfortable, with a large fallen stone as a seat. I scanned the hill and the valley below, memorizing the shadows and rock outcroppings. There would come a moment when I wouldn't be sure if a dark object were a deer or a rock—and that would be when my familiarity with the terrain would pay off.

Distantly, I heard what sounded like a dog barking.

The deer drive had begun, with the human "dogs" moving slowly up the mountain, barking as they came.

More than Man, deer fear dogs.

I don't mean giant German shepherds, or baying bloodhounds. One of the greatest dangers to the deer herd during winters of heavy snow is from ordinary household pets—terriers, beagles, Irish setters, even poodles. One dog, the leader, will pass along the farm roads and, silently, the pets will join him. Such dog packs are common in rural areas. In some counties, the game wardens are authorized to shoot them down on sight.

When the snow is deep, these ordinarily friendly dogs will pursue deer for hours, baying at their heels, until the deer are exhausted from plunging through the drifts. Sometimes the dogs attack, hamstringing the fallen deer, tearing out their intestines. Sometimes they merely circle, barking. But even then, the end result is the same. It is either death from teeth or exhaustion.

So, when men put on a drive, forcing the deer to move ahead of them in the woods toward watchers like Joan and me, they will often bay like dogs to help panic the animals.

As I said before, how like the hunting of men. How

many times have I used a partner to be the "rough tail," to follow my quarry so openly that he will be noticed? And once he has escaped the rough tail, the suspect falls easy victim to my own more subtle pursuit.

Nervously, I clicked the safety on my rifle. This was no time to draw up old memories of human hunts.

Still, they are always there, vivid and enduring. On sleepless nights they pass relentlessly before me, all those long-dead faces, those conquests in the name of duty. They do not accuse, they merely remind me of my own mortality.

The barking from the drivers was closer now.

I sensed a flicker of movement on my left, near Joan's watch. Two large does had moved out into the open field. I braced myself for the sound of her shot. Most beginners will put horns on anything that moves.

Silence. The does bounded up the slope and cleared the stone fence with easy leaps.

Joan had passed another test. She had held her fire against an easy, inviting target. I began to like her more than casually.

Now it was my turn.

He was a buck. I could tell that by the careful way he eased partially out of the wooded cover and then stopped, sniffing the air. His head was down. I sneaked my rifle up and checked him through the scope. Eight points for sure, maybe more. I made sure the safety was off and let the cross hairs move slowly down until they rested squarely two inches below the point where his swollen neck joined his heavy body. Inside the brown-haired chest was the boiler factory—the heart-lung area where a single shot would kill.

My finger caressed the trigger. A slow squeeze, and . . .

I lowered the rifle. My heart was pounding. Sweat was suddenly cold on my forehead.

Never mind, deer. Live. I don't want you for my freezer, or my mantel, either. I have had enough goddamned killing for one lifetime.

The movement of my rifle had stiffened him. Somebody once told me that deer have eyes equal to a six-power telescope. Anyway, slight as the motion had been, he had noticed it. He gathered his legs for a leap to safety.

I heard the bullet smack into his side, just milliseconds before the report of Joan's rifle reached me. He was knocked sideways, but kept on his feet. A spray of blood misted all over the snow.

She fired again, and this time he went down. All four legs went out from under him and he dropped like a falling log. He must have been dead before he hit the ground.

I saw Joan start to get up from her stand.

"Go back!" I yelled. "The drivers are coming up the hill. They may be shooting."

She faded back into the spruce trees.

Suddenly deer were running everywhere. I ducked down behind my rock. There were shots from down the hill. I heard a hit animal make a "Blat!" sound. I cursed

84

under my breath. That would be a doe. When hit, they often cry out. Not the bucks. Silently they bleed, and silently they die.

Someone had put horns onto a bare head with his imagination and eagerness to make a kill.

I heard the crunch of boots on the snow. Sam came out of the trees. He had his shotgun at the ready.

When he was within twenty feet, I gave a whistle. He froze, then relaxed. "Warren?"

I stood up. "For a minute there, it sounded like the Little Big Horn. Did you get anything?"

"Nope. Ben dropped another one, but I think it was a doe."

"It was. I heard it. How about Harry?"

"He nicked one. He's following it. There's a blood trail. What was all that shooting up this way?"

"Joan got her buck." I turned toward her watch and called, "Come on out, the war's over."

I led Sam over to the fallen animal. We bent over to examine the bullet wounds. You could have covered both of them with your hand.

"Good shooting," said Sam.

Joan joined us. "Where's your rifle?" I asked.

"I left it in the trees. I was afraid to carry it." She held out her hand. It was trembling violently. "I'd be a menace."

"I'll get it," said Sam. "Were you in the spruces?"

She nodded. He began to climb the hill.

"Well?" I asked.

She didn't have to ask, well what? Slowly, she nodded. "It was easy," she said. "So easy you wouldn't believe."

"Was it fun?"

She looked down, almost tenderly, at the dead buck. His eyes had gone milky and were glazing. Smoke rose from the bleeding wounds.

"No," she said. "I'm glad that I found out I could do it. But it's not fun at all."

8

We celebrated at Lenny's, and while the drinks were being poured, I got Sam off to one side and told him I wanted to get back to the motel. My curiosity about what waited inside that air conditioning duct was burning me up.

"I'd figured we would drive around for a couple of hours," he said.

"Sorry. Later."

His jaw clamped tightly, he shrugged and went over to put some coins in the juke box.

I collected my ginger brandy at the bar. It burned all the way down.

Joan Hartman had just concluded a deal whereby Lenny would butcher out her buck and add the meat to his Thanksgiving venison roast.

"What about the horns?" he asked.

"Let the mice eat them."

He grimaced. "I don't see where you get anything out of this deal."

Her eye caught mine. "I got everything I wanted," she said.

Harry Dassow was still up on his mountain, following a wounded buck. I had been right about the doe— naturally, it was Ben Shaw who had shot her—and he had departed for home with two carcasses in the trunk of his old Buick, their heads sticking out to observe the law that they must be "visible." Another stupid law. You can't count the hunters who proudly strap their kill to the hood of the family buggy, drive two hundred miles back to the city, and discover that in the process they have allowed the engine's heat to sour the meat beyond eating.

Shaw's doe was legal, since he had a party permit which allows the taking of one antlerless animal. But, though none of us said it out loud, such greed on opening day is not respected very much.

While Lenny and Sam were stringing Joan's buck from the tree out back, she said quietly, "How about buying me lunch?"

"Aren't you going back to Deer Creek?"

"Harry may be up on that mountain all day. He won't give up that blood trail. I don't want to sit around here."

"And you say you've known him less than a week?"

"You've known him less than a day. Do you think he will?"

"No, you're right. He'll track that buck until one of them drops."

"So I'd be stupid to wait. I want a very cold martini —stirred, not shaken—and a cheese omelette, and some blazing hot black coffee with brandy in it. What do you say?"

"I say yes."

Sam could barely keep from grumbling, because he didn't want to hunt alone, but he drove us back to my motel on the outskirts of Old Forge.

He pointed out to Joan, "You know, you're getting further and further away from home."

"Warren will take care of me. Won't you?"

"You bet," I said, zinging Sam.

He made little gnashing sounds, but he deposited us safely at the motel, refused my offer to buy him a drink, and ordered me to appear for dinner that night in case our paths did not cross in the meanwhile.

"Does Jenny have any surprise guest tonight?" I asked.

He started to make a wisecrack, looked at Joan and decided against it. "Just family."

"Okay," I said.

He ground gears and drove off in a spray of flying slush.

"Your buddy's mad," said Joan.

"He's got the right to be. I came up here to hunt with him—he planned on it—and now I'm letting him down."

"All for little me?"

"Don't get cutey pie, Miss Montana. I've got other things to do today."

"Oh? Did your wife arrive unexpectedly?"

"What's that supposed to mean?"

She touched the ring. It's beaten silver, but it doesn't take many brains to tell that it's a wedding band, even if it is on my right hand, European-style.

"I respect you for wearing it. I meet so many men who take it off and then everyone can see the white streak around their finger where they aren't tanned. It's all so tawdry."

"You sound like a young lady of considerable experience."

"I've been around," she said, tossing her salt-and-pepper hair.

"I'll bet," I said, slapping her rump. "All the way from Cut Bank down to Helena, Montana!"

She gave a little yelp that was half protest, half pleasure, and we went into the bar and ordered her a very dry martini—stirred, not shaken, just the way James Bond used to drink them.

On the pretext of hitting the john, I slipped outside and beat it down to my room. My outside indicators were still intact, but I didn't put too much trust in them and went in fast and low. The room was empty, and apparently undisturbed.

It took me thirty seconds to remove the air conditioning grate. My cigarette ash indicators were still there, but somebody had been inside anyway. My gear hadn't been bothered, but now there was the addition of a small package wrapped in brown paper. I used my hunting knife to slit open one corner, and saw a hundred-dollar bill peeking back at me.

There were ninety of them. Nine thousand dollars. And a brief note:

THIS BUYS A LOT OF TIME ON THE MACHINE. GO HOME.

I fingered the bills. The note was right. At three thousand dollars a month, this little package meant three months of hospital bills.

I put the money in my suitcase. There wasn't any place in the room where I could hide it that would be safe from professional search, so why bother?

As for my gear, I distributed it among the pockets I'd had sewn into my quilted hunting vest. The one exception was the .357 Magnum. I slipped it down inside my trousers into a specially padded pocket that made it nearly invisible to the casual eye.

The pistol looked like any other pistol. The ammunition looked like any other ammunition. But both assumptions would have been quite wrong.

The gun itself was made of high-density plastic, springs and all. There wasn't a gram of metal in it. The same was true of the ammunition, with the exception of the non-ferrous soft lead slugs. The shell casings were of the same super-strong plastic; the primer caps were made of a softer plastic. Nothing about the pistol or its load would cause the slightest tickle of a metal detector.

I had carried this weapon through so many airport security checkpoints that it was eligible for membership in the Admiral's Club.

Of course, at such times, I have always been very careful not to have anything else on my person that might set off the alarm. It would be really stupid to get stopped for my metal Playboy Club card, and have a search reveal the .357.

I looked at the note again. It was printed in block letters. Small chance of handwriting analysis.

Nine thousand dollars. Not a fortune, but like the man said, three more months of life for Alice.

At that moment, I realized that I had fully decided to take the money and go home. Why not? I had no personal involvement in whatever it was that had been going on up here. I had reacted violently that morning, when attacked. But now that I had calmed down, wasn't it smart to take the money and run? I had worked much harder for less.

The big question now was, would they let me skip out after having lamed one of their men?

Well, we would see.

I took the hotel ball-point pen and wrote a note of my own on an envelope.

Good idea. I'm on my way.

I propped it up against the TV set's rabbit ears. Maybe the right eyes would see it.

•　　•　　•

Joan Hartman was starting her second martini.

"We thought you had fallen in," she said.

"We?"

"You've got a visitor. Drink up. You may need it."

I sipped at my Scotch. "I went back to the room for some dry socks."

"Lucky you. My toes are turning numb."

"Did you order lunch?"

"No. I don't think you're going to have time to eat any."

"Why not?"

She nodded toward the bar door. "He's why not. I guess they just went to your room too."

"He" was Sheriff Oscar Deep, and with him were two deputies, and none of them were smiling.

Naturally, they refused drinks.

The Sheriff said, "Stone, I've got a complaint on you."

"For what?"

"Story is, you shot a man in the leg this morning."

"Whose story?"

"Two fellers from Birmingham, Alabama. They say they were hunting up on the state land, and you tried to run them off from where you were still-hunting. When they argued, you plugged one of them in the ankle. Is that what happened?"

I felt the surge of blood to my head, the call to action. But I kept my body still and my voice calm. "Yes and no," I said.

He sighed. "I kind of hoped you'd say it was somebody else. Maybe you'd better come on down to the office with us."

"Are you arresting me, Sheriff?"

"Not unless you insist. Why don't you come in friend-ly-like, and we'll talk."

"No. We're having lunch, this lady and me, and then I have to drive her home. Afterwards, I'll come by and talk with you. Friendly-like."

"We'd rather do it now."

"Then put on the cuffs," I said. "You'll have to make an arrest."

As the words fell, stupidly, from my mouth, I remembered the hardware in my hunting vest, and the pistol in my waistband. But it was too late.

In New York, they have what they call the Sullivan law, which will put you away for a year for merely possessing an unlicensed handgun. For an ordinary citizen to have a license is in the same category as his getting permission to spend the night with the governor's wife. It hadn't even occurred to me to try and get one.

The two deputies moved toward me. I slipped back, away from them.

"Hey, Sheriff, I was only kidding about the cuffs. I'll come along." I had shrugged out of my vest, and I handed it to the surprised Joan Hartman. "You better wear this, kid. It's cold up on that mountain." I tossed her my van keys. "You can drive my van. I'll pick it up later in Deer Creek." The deputies had hesitated, and before they could move toward me again, I grabbed

94

Joan and embraced her like a bear. "Let's have a kiss."

Amazed, she let me kiss her, and during our embrace, I managed to jam the pistol down the back of her hunting pants. She felt it, of course, but other than stiffening slightly, she gave no other sign.

I moved away from her fast, slapped the Sheriff on the arm, and said, "Let's go."

9

I sat in the back of the patrol car, with an iron grid between me and the driver. Both deputies were up front. Sheriff Deep rode with me.

"You were nearly plumb foolish back there," he said.

"You caught me by surprise. I was getting ready to go to bed."

His bushy eyebrows rose. "I thought you said you were going to have lunch with that young lady."

"What did you expect me to say?"

He chuckled. "That's a good-looking woman," he admitted. "Damn it, Stone, you had me worried. Why didn't you just come along peaceful? Sam Keith's a good friend of mine. You must know that I didn't want to roust you."

"Sheriff, it's okay. I've been meaning to talk with you anyway. But don't tell me that you believe that phony

96

story those guys gave you. Not after the way I was shot at last night."

"If you were in the right, why didn't you come on in and report it?"

"Because we were hunting. Anyway, I did mention it."

"Where?"

"To Ben Shaw."

That was the wrong name to use. The Sheriff hawked, lowered his window, and spat out into the wind.

"Ben's got no authority over here."

"I know that. But what I was trying to show is that I wasn't trying to hush up what happened."

"No, I guess you weren't. Okay, Stone. Give me your version."

I did, with the exception of the proof we'd found that the man had been hit. I didn't mention the package of money, either.

He scowled. "They just told you to shove off, no reason given?"

"Not a hint."

"Why would they do that? What do you have to do with a couple of out-of-state hunters from Alabama?"

"Five to one they're not from Alabama. I know they weren't hunters. They were greenhorns in the woods. My guess they're mixed up in some way with those hanged men, and they believe that I had something to do with hanging them."

"Why would they think something awful nasty like that?"

"Come on, Sheriff. You know who I am, and what I do."

He nodded slowly. "Yeah, I have to admit that we checked you out. All right, Stone. *Did* you?"

"Did I what?"

"Did you hang them three gangsters from those tree limbs?"

"Hell, no! But I suppose you don't believe me."

He shook his head. "You're wrong, old buddy. I believe you."

"Why? Because of my honest face?"

"Nope. And if you want the truth, your face isn't all that honest. I believe you because it isn't your style, not from what I've been told. And I'll tell you something else. I believe you about those two hunters, too." He lowered the window and spat again, then tapped on the metal grid. "Hey, Roy! Call in and tell Marty to hold them two fellers from Alabama."

"Right," said the deputy on the passenger side. He started mumbling into the two-way radio.

"What puzzles me," said Deep, "is why they came in at all, especially if their identification wouldn't hold up. They must have known they'd have to run long before I'd get you locked up."

"How badly did I shoot him?"

"Mighty painful. You took a chunk out of his anklebone. He ain't going to play split end no more, that's for sure."

"There's your answer. They had to get him to a hospital. Hospitals report gunshot wounds. They figured it

98

was safer to let you in on the act, so the hospital wouldn't be suspicious. Once he got fixed up, they'd run like hell."

The deputy up front turned around and said, "Sheriff, Marty says they took the wounded man over to the Old Forge hospital."

Deep swore. "Who took them? When?"

More mumbling on the radio, then, "Miss Jackson drove them over about half an hour ago."

"Laura? Why her?"

"Marty says we were short-handed and couldn't spare an officer."

I asked, "Why didn't they drive themselves?"

"They said their car was parked up too far for them to walk to it, so they hitched a ride down the mountain."

"So you don't even have a license number."

"I know. Roy, put in a call to Old Forge hospital. Get the duty man there. Have those two held until we arrive."

"On what charge?"

"How the hell do I know? Malicious destruction of Christmas trees. Anything. Just detain them."

He sat back glumly. After a while, he said, "One of their buddies drove them over, and then took the car back to the hospital to wait. Sneaky."

"Am I in custody?" I asked.

"No. But don't bother me."

"Can I go to the hospital with you? I would like very much to talk with those two."

"Where do you think we're going now? Patterson, get this heap turned around and let's mainline it to the hospital!" I opened my mouth, and he said, "Shut up. Let me think."

I shut up. He thought.

We were too late. The wounded man had been treated and released. Laura was still at the hospital, filling out forms. She was surprised to see the Sheriff, even more surprised to see me.

"Are you all right?" I asked.

"All right? Of course. Why not?"

Standing close to her, I got a slight scent of chocolate. It made me smile.

Deep explained the situation. Laura nodded. "I didn't really buy their story."

I said, "I'm glad somebody trusts me."

"Oh, it's not that. I never doubted that you shot him. But merely to protect your hunting stand? The mind boggles."

"What names did they use?" I asked.

"The one you shot said he was Charlie Roberts. The other one was Fred Chapman. I think the first names were probably correct. At least, they answered to them."

"Didn't you see any I.D.?"

"Only their hunting licenses. They checked out. They said they'd left their wallets at the hotel for safe-keeping."

Deep asked, "What hotel?"

"The Oneida, right here in Old Forge."

"Roy, check that out."

Laura turned back to her forms. I glowered at the Sheriff. He scowled back and said, "Okay. So I jumped the gun a little."

"A little? It seems to me that you went rushing out with your whole force following you to pick up Big Bad Warren, while you left all of the basic investigation to Laura."

"Guilty as sin," he admitted. "Hell, it looked open and shut. I didn't really buy all of their story, either, but at the very least it looked like you might have been responsible for an accident. Come on, I'll make up for it by buying you that lunch you missed with your girl friend."

This earned me a hard look from Laura. "I thought you were out on the freezing mountain, hunting the wary white-tail. Four-legged, that is."

I tried for a joke. "All hunting and no lunch makes Jack a—"

She sniffed and turned away.

Deep punched my arm. "Come on. I ain't got all day."

"I'll call you later," I told Laura as we left. She did not bother to answer.

Outside, I said, "Sheriff, did anybody ever tell you that you have a very large mouth?"

"Sorry, boy. How was I supposed to know you had *two* of them on the string? My God, you only been in town one day."

"I like Laura," I said. "She's not on any string."

He clapped his hand over his mouth. "Shooting it off again. Here, this is the place."

We went up three wooden steps and into what looked like a pool hall with frosted windows, and the name JOE'S painted in red. Inside, there were, indeed, three pool tables, actively surrounded by men dressed for hunting.

"They won't shoot many deer in here," I said.

The Sheriff laughed. "They don't expect to. It gets them out of the house, though. Along about sundown, they'll all hit the road and ride around long enough to drink a six-pack. A couple of them, believe it or not, *will* stumble over some dumb buck and drop him. More likely, they'll shoot a doe. After a six-pack or two, these good boys can put horns on a tree stump."

"Beer?" he added, as we found space at the end of the bar.

I nodded. "What is it you want to talk about, Sheriff?"

He held up two fingers. "Do you like sausage? Good hot Polish sausage? You'd better, because that's all that Joe serves."

"Sounds good."

The beers came, and he said, "Two kielbasi, Joe. Hot."

"Some onions?" asked Joe.

"Shoot the works."

I sipped my Utica Club. "Come on, Sheriff. Get to the bottom line."

"Okay. By now, Stone, you must have realized that

102

you're in deep waters."

"I sort of got that message. I've been shot at, threatened, and my room's been searched."

He snapped his fingers. "I didn't think you'd catch us."

"Oh? You've been in there too?"

"Too? You've had more than one search?"

"Sheriff, I've had several. What did *you* find?"

"Nothing incriminating. Which didn't surprise me. Your reputation precedes you, Stone, like a big wind precedes a storm. Frankly, I've never bought that story about you and Sam Keith hunting our white-tailed deer, delicious though they may be. Hell, you can hunt anyplace you want."

"Right. But I wanted to hunt here."

He spread both hands. "Maybe. But what happens the day after you arrive? Three men are found hanging from trees. Stone, until you showed up, we never had men hanging from our trees."

"It's a first for me, too," I said.

"I know it's not your style," he said. "You do it more low key. But face it, when you bust a town, you bust it for keeps. That land shark out in Arizona, the one who bilked all those old folks with his retirement village? He's never been seen since his suckers hired you to pay him a visit."

"He got wandering feet," I said. "Luckily, I managed to convince him to return most of the money before he split."

"Yeah. If you ask me, those wandering feet led him

103

to a desert sinkhole somewhere. Come on, Stone, tell me that those two Cubans who were running that murder and robbery ring in Venice, Florida, just happened to stroll into a river full of alligators."

"That's what the coroner put in his report. They were probably lost."

"Bull!" He slammed his beer can down so hard that it spouted foam all the way up to the ceiling. Everybody stopped what they were doing and looked at us. He raised his voice even louder. "Syracuse can take Buffalo any day of the week!"

That calmed the natives. Football is plenty of reason for the slamming of beer cans. They went back to their pool games.

"Back there in your car, Sheriff, you said you believed me when I told you I didn't have anything to do with those hanged men."

"Damn it, I *do* believe you. That's the hell of it."

"Why?"

"Because if you didn't do it, somebody around here did, and I don't like to start thinking about who it might be."

The Polish sausage, fried to a rich brown and buried in deliciously greasy onions and green peppers, was a delight. It called for more beer, and Joe was quick to answer the call.

"Try this," he said, shoving two golden cans at us. "Matt's. It's the real thing."

I inhaled half a can, and choked. It was, indeed, the

real thing. Joe laughed and said, "That's the best stuff you can get around here, unless the boys smuggle down some LaBatt from Canada."

When he went back down the bar, I said to Deep, "Come on, Sheriff. You still haven't gotten to that bottom line. Why are you walking all around it?"

"It ain't something I like to hit a man with on an empty stomach."

I patted my gut. "After Joe's sausage? It may be burning, but it's not empty."

"Okay," he said. "It's about your lady friend. Not Laura. The other one. Joan Hartman."

"What have you got on her?"

"Did you ever hear of Vince Hartman?"

"The Enforcer? Hell, yes. Who hasn't?"

He ticked off the points on his fingers. "Accused of nineteen hits. Beat the rap every time. And for every time he was accused, you can add another three contracts the law never heard about. For twenty years, he had the FBI running in circles. He used to write letters to J. Edgar Hoover, for God's sake, kidding him about the way the agents kept goofing up. Well, Vince dropped out of sight around three years ago. Our hunch is that somebody finally put him under."

"Small loss. But what's his connection to Joan?"

"She's his daughter."

It jolted me. I drank some beer to cover my reaction.

He went on: "Back in the fifties, she was taken out west by her mother."

"Divorce?"

"No. I'm not sure of the reasons, but she and Vince stayed on good terms. He sent money, visited every now and then. Maybe she just got fed up with the mob life, and he was man enough to let her go. You've got to give him credit for that."

"Why not? Everybody, even the bad guys, has problems and a family. But how is it Joan's fault that her father was a hit man?"

"It isn't. But her showing up here right now is one hell of a coincidence."

"Why?"

"Because the last time Vince Hartman was ever seen alive was up at Judge Dassow's mansion, during that Syndicate convention."

He drove me back to my motel. On the way, we saw three deer near the road. One was a handsome buck.

I laughed. "And neither of us with a rifle. Don't you hunt, Sheriff?"

"Not any more. Most of my men do, and they leave a little meat off at the house. I've shot enough deer to know that I can do it. What's the point in killing any more?"

I stared out at the ice-clad road. "Yeah, I know what you mean."

"I figured you would. Warren, I ain't meddling, but your wife's situation showed up in our checkout. How long do you think you can handle that?"

"As long as I have to."

"It sure doesn't leave you much for yourself."

"I get by."

"Did you ever think of going into regular law enforcement? You'd be good at it."

I laughed. There was a sour taste in my mouth. "What kind of regular job would give me forty thousand a year just for hospital bills?"

"You'd be surprised at the good deals we can finagle for dependents. They slice off the overhead, and that saves you a good seventy percent of what you'd pay otherwise."

"At a state hospital? No thanks, Sheriff."

"Some of them are damned good. At least, up here."

I stared at him. "Oscar, our state hospitals in Kentucky are just as good if not better than any you've got in your damned northeast corridor. But the man with the cash register is the man who calls the tune. I don't intend to turn that power over to anybody. This is my show. So I have to foot the whole bill. It's worth it."

Deep shrugged. "Just trying to help."

"I know. Everybody wants to help. But they can't. *You* can't, Sheriff. Thanks anyway."

"Don't mention it."

The radio squawked. He pressed the mike button. "Yeah?"

"Sheriff, those two skipped out of their hotel a few minutes before we got there. There was a third man with them, according to the manager. They all registered as from Birmingham."

"Okay," said the Sheriff. "Keep me posted."

We pulled into the motel parking lot. My battered

van was still there.

Deep didn't get out of the patrol car. "I'll put out an APB on those characters. Meanwhile, I'd appreciate it if you'd keep me posted on Miss Hartman."

"You've got to be kidding."

"I leveled with *you,* Stone."

"Quid pro quo?"

"What the hell does that mean?"

"You scratch my back and I'll scratch yours. Well, I didn't sign on to spy on my friends for you, Sheriff. Sorry."

"Damn it, I didn't say spy. But if you see her getting in any trouble, it might help her if I knew about it."

"Let's leave it at this, Sheriff. I'll think it over."

He muttered something, and kicked the squad car into gear.

Joan wasn't in the bar, but she *was* waiting in my room.

"I was just getting ready to drive away when I saw the maid coming in," she told me. "So I scuttled inside and told her I was Mrs. Stone. Now they'll probably charge you for a double." She sniffed. "From that mess on your bathroom mirror, I'd say it's only fair."

"Snoopy."

She lifted one of the pillows. The .357 Magnum was under it.

"I take it you don't have a permit for this odd contraption," she said. "Which is why you slid it down my derriere."

"Right. And many thanks. That was life's most embarrassing moment."

She indicated my hunting vest, which was draped over the back of a chair. "And what about that little beauty? Who exactly *are* you, Warren Stone? Secret Agent X-9?"

"I'm kind of a free-lance vigilante. When a town gets in trouble, they hire me to bail them out."

"From all the equipment you carry, I'd guess you're good at your work."

"Good enough. But don't get me wrong, Joan. I don't work the same side of the street as Vince Hartman."

She squeezed her eyes closed. No tears came out. But I knew they were contained within.

"That lunkhead of a Sheriff told you?"

"Yes. But don't be so quick to write him off as a lunkhead. He might surprise you."

"You're right. I suppose he's got a theory about why I'm here."

"He knows that your father disappeared here three years ago."

"I *think* he did. It's hard to be sure. Until last year, his—associates—kept us quiet with a large chunk of manure on how he was out of the country, ducking an indictment. They delivered letters he was supposed to have written. But they didn't sound like him."

"He and your mother were separated?"

"Since 1957. But she always loved him. It was just that she couldn't accept what—he did."

"And you?"

"I only saw him a few times. He was gruff and distant.

109

He always brought presents, but he didn't have the slightest idea of what a little girl would really want. Once, he brought me a book bag. A book bag, for God's sake! I used it for picking blackberries."

"Who led you to believe he was overseas?"

"The 'boys.' Isn't that what you call them? It was always a different group. They'd drive up in their big black cars, with their little black briefcases. Sometimes they brought a check for Mama, although it usually came by mail. And there were always papers for her to sign. Apparently he had put lots of things in her name. We were too dumb to see through their scheme. Once she had signed all the papers—that took more than a year—we never saw them again. Or the checks. They just stopped coming."

"Then what?"

"We wrote letters. They came back. We didn't dare go to the police. What could we have told them? That my gangster father had apparently skipped out on us? They would have laughed us right out of the station house. So we just drifted along. We were careful, there was enough to live on. And I worked in the Bureau of Indian Affairs. We got by."

"Until?"

"Mama died in June. During the summer, I made friends with a couple who were touring around the country in a camper. They live in Deer Creek, and in talking about this area, they happened to mention the big crime convention that had been held here. It was the first I'd heard of it. The time relationship struck me, so I researched it. I found out that my father was one of the people picked up and questioned. And I knew that after that week, we had never heard from him again, assuming those letters were forgeries."

"So you decided to come east."

"Yes. It never occurred to me that anyone would connect my name with his, or I would have used another one. You're right, Sheriff Deep is anything but a lunkhead."

"All right, you're here. Now what?"

"Now I'm going to find my father. He's here somewhere, I know."

"Where?"

Her voice broke. "Underground, I suppose. He's dead. They must have killed him. That's the only thing that could have happened." She looked directly at me, and her eyes seemed to blaze in the gloom of the curtained motel room. "If so, I don't know how, but I'll find whoever did it and drop him in his tracks."

Softly, I said, "So that's why you had to shoot that deer this morning?"

"Yes. I wanted to see if I could take a life and watch the blood flow. Now I know, I can."

My voice sounded a thousand years old as I said, "And I wish that was one lesson you'd never learned."

10

She was willing to make love, but I couldn't. She was too vulnerable. What small comfort it might have brought her wasn't worth the guilt we would both have felt later. So I held her in my arms, and listened as she talked about her home, and her mother, and her unwilling love for the stranger who was her father.

I tried to blunt the raw edge of her anger, because it would be harmful to her. If her father *had* been murdered, and she wanted to destroy that murderer, that was her business. But the way she was now, she would never succeed, and would only become another victim herself.

She never asked me for help, and I didn't offer it. After a long while, she stopped talking and just lay in the warm bed with me, nested very small against my body. She had stopped shivering, and her breath came softly as if she were asleep. I knew she wasn't. But if she wanted to pretend, that was fine with me.

In a little while, her voice calm, she said, "What is all that stuff in your hunting vest? You look like a hardware store."

"Little gadgets to make my life easier. And maybe longer. The glass balls contain various kinds of gas. Tear gas. Another gas that puts people to sleep for ten minutes. A couple of smoke bombs."

"No nerve gas?"

"Not this trip."

"Meaning that you've used it on other occasions?"

I thought back to some of my zap squad missions. Still, I had never actually *used* the stuff then, although I had been ready to. So I wasn't really lying when I told her, "No."

"How about all those little tools, what are they?"

"Picks for locks. Wire tapping gadgets. Pep pills. All the conveniences of modern life."

"No knockout pills?"

"Those too."

She sat up. "Do you know what they call a man like you out our way? One mean hombre."

"Hombre is further south."

"We learned it from a Paul Newman movie."

"You must be feeling better."

She smoothed back her hair. "Some. Hey, that was some nice feeling, all that comfort from your strong, manly arms."

Something in her voice grated on my nerves. "Don't

113

poison it, Joan. You haven't been rejected. All you really wanted today was somebody to hang onto until the boat quit rocking. Okay, I think the water's calm now. So how about that lunch you missed?"

She was angry with herself for having opened up to me so completely, so she was spoiling for a fight. I didn't give her a chance to open fire. I went into the bathroom, splashed myself with cold water, waited while she freshened up, and then we went to buy her an omelette.

I didn't know why I trusted this tall girl from Montana, but I did, so as she ate, I brought her up to date on what had been happening here in the snow-filled Adirondacks since my arrival yesterday.

I finished, "Everything seems to keep coming back to that Syndicate meeting three years ago. Nobody seems to know why they gathered. It must have been something big for them to take the risk. But whatever they had planned, the raid cut it short."

"But nobody was arrested."

"No. They got rousted on a lot of minor charges, but there wasn't anything the law could make stick. Still, there must have been a lot of license plate switching once those boys got home."

"What do you mean?"

I told her about the way the federal agents had photographed all of the license plates.

She nodded. "Yes, they even used to do that to me

when I'd go to a drive-in movie with some boy. They never came out in the open against Mom and me, but we always knew they were around."

"That's their style. Let's get back to now. Here we've got the memory of a big to-do that got busted up before it accomplished whatever it was being held for. So time passes. Three years, to be exact."

"Three years during which," she added bitterly, "my father has been missing."

"Right. And during which somebody burns down the Dassow mansion. Why? To destroy evidence?"

She considered. "Maybe. Or to uncover some?"

"How's that?"

"Suppose something were hidden in that house, something nobody had been able to find. Maybe, in desperation, they just lit a torch in hopes that something would show up."

"Could be. But what did they expect to find?"

She spread her hands. "That's the end of my womanly intuition."

"Okay. Let's say that something may have been hidden. It probably hasn't been found yet, or there still wouldn't be all this heat. What bothers me is that it seems to be aimed right at me. Here I blunder into town, fat, dumb and happy, and the next thing I know, my room is being searched by experts, I'm shot at in a friendly warning way, and this morning two toughs ambush me and tell me to get out or else."

She looked down into her coffee. "You look as if you

115

could handle most of the 'or elses' they might come up with."

"Don't take odds. Kid, we all have soft spots. When they come at me head-on, like that bird did this morning, I'll take my chances on being able to survive. But—"

"But they might be able to strike at you through someone else?"

"That's what the nasty man hinted."

"So you shot him."

"I shot *at* him. Joan, I've got years of practice making what I call 'sound shots.' " Her face darkened, and I laughed. "Simmer down, I don't mean your stupid hunter's sound shot, blazing away at the snap of a twig. But in my business, it helps if I can spot the location of a sound in the darkness, or if it comes from behind cover. So I practice. Down in Kentucky, I set up cheap two-buck speakers outside in the night and feed sounds into them from a cassette player. I'm good enough to hit a four-inch speaker three times out of four without ever being able to see it."

"All right. You shot *at* him. And hit him in the ankle."

"He had a gun on me. I didn't try to hit his ankle. I didn't try *not* to hit it, either. He got unlucky, that's all."

"Then what?"

"I came back here honestly prepared to leave today for Kentucky."

She was surprised by that. "You'd let them run you off?"

"Why not? I doubt that there's anything personal between us. But somehow, just by being here, I represented a threat. They warned me about that, and they were prepared to pay for my inconvenience. Why shouldn't I take their money and go home? Who needs trouble?"

"I thought that was your business, trouble."

"Only when I'm hired for it. Who hired me to get myself shot at up here?"

She looked away. I touched her hand.

"Joan, I know you're thinking about your father. But that's got nothing to do with me. I'm a stranger here myself, remember?"

"But you're involved. You found those others, the three hanged men."

"I helped find *one* of them. I didn't put him in that tree, and I don't have anything to do with him."

"And you don't even care who did?"

"Only as it affects me, or someone close to me."

"So you're just going to walk away?"

"That's what looks like the smartest thing for me to do."

She pushed her cup away. Her voice trembled. "All right, Mr. Hired Vigilante. You do what's smart and profitable!"

"Where are you going?"

"To call Harry Dassow. I need a ride home."

"I'll drive you in the van."

She told me what I could do with my blue van. It was impossible.

I left her dialing the pay phone. So I've got a temper, too.

The note I'd left on top of the TV set was gone.

So was the nine thousand dollars.

11

Paranoia lives inside all of us. It doesn't take much to call it to the surface.

Okay, I'd been robbed.

Notice how I had assumed possession of that money, although it really didn't belong to me until I had fulfilled the obligation it was intended to pay for? Once the green stuff is in your hand, it seems to stick there.

It seemed logical to assume that Charlie Roberts and Fred Chapman, or whatever their real names were, had gotten mad at me for plugging one of them, and had called off their offer.

On the other hand, Miss Joan Hartman, of Cut Bank, Montana, had been in my room alone long enough to find the cash and stash it someplace nearby for later pickup. Or it might even be in her pockets. I didn't like to think this about her, but I did, what with my newly surfaced paranoia, so I hightailed it out of my room and back up to the bar-restaurant.

Joan wasn't there, and neither the bartender nor the waitress could remember when she'd left. It was recently, since I had only been gone four or five minutes.

I went out and looked up and down the highway. She wasn't anywhere in sight. I stood on the white center line to see if she were hitchhiking on the shoulder, but I didn't spot her.

A horn sent me back onto the motel parking lot in one leap. It was Sam in his jeep.

"Are you hunting right down the middle of the main highway?" he asked.

"Just sightseeing. How about a beer?"

He shivered. "Make that a ginger brandy."

We went into the bar. "Get your business finished?" he asked.

"More or less. Do you want to hunt the rest of the afternoon?"

"That's why I'm here. I saw a couple we could have had, with two men on their trail."

"All right." We toasted—he with his glass of ginger brandy, and me with my can of Utica Club. "Will we be hitching up with anyone else?"

"Maybe Ben Shaw."

"Him? He's already shot two today."

"One on his wife's tag, and the doe on the party permit. Ben's still got his own license to go."

"Ben's a real conservationist," I said.

"Don't be too hard on him. He needs the meat. They

don't pay him more than ten thousand a year over there in Hamilton County."

"Is that a valid reason to play the hog? Why doesn't he hunt liquor stores? One caper there is worth a dozen deer."

Sam was mad. He finished knocking his brandy back in one jolt.

"What the hell do you know?" he coughed. "Oh, you've got your own problems. But you're still playing in the top games, for the big thou."

"Explain that, Sam."

"Sure. You deal in thousands, not hundreds. But to some of us, there are still a hundred pennies in every dollar. When the store prices bacon at one-twenty-nine, that's still a penny cheaper than a buck-thirty. Ben buys his oil at Carl's, even if it may not be as good as Gulf's top line. Why? Because it's fourteen cents a quart cheaper, my friend. He's also got two kids in high school. They don't drive hot rods, they don't go to Vail for ski vacations. They fish for the frying pan, and they trap muskrat for movie money. So where do you, with your twenty-thousand-dollar fees, get off badmouthing him because he takes as many deer for his table as he's legally entitled?"

Twenty thousand. So he had overheard all my conversation with Mayor Borkh. How much else had he filed away on me during these two days? And why?

I looked at him closely. This was still Sam Keith, my friend, in whose hands I had placed my life more than once.

And yet, he wasn't Sam any more, either. He was sweating, and that was not Sam. There was a tense set to his lips that wasn't Sam, either.

I wanted to ask him, "Why?" But this wasn't the time.

Instead, I said, "Sorry. I guess I just wasn't seeing the whole picture. Well, are we going to drink, or are we going to hunt?"

In my room, with Sam outside warming up the jeep, I saw something I'd missed before.

Joan Hartman had left her .308 Winchester leaning in the corner. I snapped open the bolt. A live round spilled out onto the bed. She had one demerit coming, for bringing a loaded rifle inside. I emptied the remaining three rounds and tossed them into an ash tray. Then I took my own gear and went out to meet Sam.

"Did Dassow ever find his deer?" I asked, as we drove up toward Bear Paw.

"Not that I heard of. Last report, he'd gone over the top into the next valley. Some friend of Ben's saw him."

We drove in silence for a while. Then he said, "I'm sorry for taking off on you back there about Ben."

"Forget it."

"No. I was wrong. You put the right name on him. He *is* a hog. He drops everything he gets in his sights, whether or not he needs the meat. He's the kind of louse who gets into a flock of quail and kills them all, leaving nothing for seed. He doesn't break the law, not that I know of, but he sure as hell stretches it out as far

122

as it'll go." He spat out the open side of the jeep. "I guess it was really *me* I was bitching about. Maybe I'm jealous of you."

"Of me? You've got to be kidding."

He waved one hand. "Oh, not about Alice. Buddy, that's more burden than one mortal man should bear. No, not that. But in spite of her, you still move around pretty good. You're still in action, you make big money, you go good places, you have *fun!*"

I thought about what he'd just said. Fun? Well, maybe. The normal person wouldn't consider the tension and danger of a hard assignment as fun. But neither Sam nor I were normal persons. I decided he was entitled to use the word.

"Sam," I probed, "don't you like the gun shop any more?"

"Like it? I hate every minute there! It's a nickel and dime way of living. I know weapons, but who wants to pay for that? They want it delivered yesterday, and they want it cheap. Never mind about good workmanship."

"So pack it in. Do something else."

"Sure." He hit his stiff leg with a clenched fist. "Maybe sign on as night watchman at Sheffield Chemicals?"

"Screw you, friend. If what you want is tender, loving care, you picked the wrong guy. I'm sorry you're down in the dumps, but this self-pity act leaves me cold."

He shifted down into second with a savage ripping of gears and shot off the main road onto a steep trail that climbed up the mountain.

"The hell with this road-hunting," he growled. "Let's go find one that'll make us work."

We found one.

My glasses showed a full, basket-shaped rack that went ten points for sure. The buck was sheltered under a stand of apple trees that had gone wild from their former domestic existence as the orchard of some German immigrant farmer whose heirs had long since made their own immigration to the industrial wastelands of the city. Now—unpruned and untended—the fruit had become small and bitter, fit only for deer fodder.

The distance, more than four hundred yards, was too long for a safe killing shot.

"Take him," said Sam. "I'll stand watch up here. If you go along the road maybe a hundred yards, there's a draw that'll bring up on the side hill above him."

"You sure you don't want him? That's a nice rack."

"With this leg? I'd never get within shooting distance."

I slipped out of the jeep. "Okay. If I drop him, I'll give you three quick shots so you can come up and help drag him out. If *that's* not too rough for your poor crippled leg."

He laughed. "I guess I can make it. Given time and enough ginger brandy." He handed me the flask. "One for the climb?"

I sipped at it, felt the hot liquid burning down my throat. "Thanks."

"Warren—"

"Yeah?"

He swallowed whatever he'd been about to say. "Oh, hell."

I punched his shoulder. "You're forgiven. Save me some of that brandy."

"Not to worry. I've got a whole fifth in the glove."

As I crunched up the snow-covered road, I loaded up my rifle. I kept looking off to the right for the ravine he'd mentioned. Once, when I thought I had found it, I wasted ten minutes in learning that it faded away to nothing.

The genuine draw, when I approached it, left no doubt. It had been carved by centuries of water cascading down the mountain during the spring thaws. I checked the safety on the Ought-six, held onto a tree to let myself onto the steep banks, and began the slow chore of sneaking up on the unsuspecting buck.

The woods are what you make of them. If you crash through them heedlessly, they become an entrapping nest of branches and hidden footfalls. If you roar through them on your trail bike, they are as barren of wildlife as any Sahara. If you jangle the air with your portable radio, you might as well be trekking through Times Square.

But if you move carefully, observing your surroundings with care and respect, if you place each foot so it will not disturb the fallen leaves and twigs, or mar the always-changing map of the forest floor, you will soon become neighbor with a teeming habitat of birds and animals who are willing to accept you into their world so long as you behave yourself.

I took my time. Nothing is more wasteful in the forest than hurrying. There is a gentle ebb and flow of movement there, and if you want to become part of the woods, you must sense the cycles of the wind and the wildlife, and adapt yourself to them.

But, because I am a predator, a hunter, I need an extra instinct: an awareness of my own impact on the forest. No action is without reaction; my job as hunter is to limit my own actions to avoid alerting my quarry.

It had been the same that July morning seven years ago in Vienna, when I pretended to stalk a Russian defector who had sold us phony lists of Western sympathizers in Warsaw. To my partner—who was actually a double agent who didn't know that his dual role had been blown weeks before—my every move, my every glance, seemed concentrated on the Russian.

And there was another game that even I didn't know about. No mere double cross, this was at least a triple betrayal. Someone in Moscow wanted the Russian defector dead, so they'd set him up to be hit by our side. Meanwhile, somebody else wanted *me* dead, so they had planted the double agent on me as a partner. But somebody else had jumped the gun, wanting to be rid of the double, and so I was forewarned.

At the morning's end, the good-bye pile contained

126

only one double agent who had been unlucky enough to make his move too soon, short-circuiting my own plans for taking him alive. The Russian defector had departed for parts unknown, and I got another blue card in my file.

The blue cards were important. You added one every time you had to terminate someone. Allen Dulles had decided, long ago, that the more times you killed, the more vulnerable you became. Far from practice making perfect, his theory was that killing put an agent into blue moods, depression, and eventual unreliability.

I had accumulated eight blue cards by the time I walked into the office of Special Prosecutor Archibald Cox and told him what I knew about Watergate. By that evening, another agent had been instructed to add a blue card to his file. Instead, I added one more to my own file. If they were still keeping tabs on me by then.

The next time they sent somebody after me, I returned him with a broken arm and a message: Watergate was only the tip of the iceberg of information I had stashed away. I promised that my death, even under the most ordinary of circumstances, would result in that information being mailed by a trusted friend to the editors of the gray old lady of journalism, *The New York Times.*

The faceless ones in Washington countered with open threats against my wife.

I laughed at them. While my life is, and will be, devoted to preserving her, any removal of that responsibility would be the most welcome thing that ever happened. So, realizing what a weak straw they grasped, the faceless ones backed off, leaving Alice—along with her three thousand dollars a month in hospital bills—to me.

All right. I could handle it.

I had to.

12

The wind was in my face, so I was able to get close to the buck without him scenting me.

He had seen the jeep, though, and was watching it carefully. His head was up, and the antlers were magnificent. I glassed him through my rifle scope. His coat was a rich brown, untainted by patches of falling hair.

I laid the cross hairs just behind his flicking ears, where the spinal column stiffened the heavy neck, and slipped off my safety.

Once again, the soft sadness descended over me, and I found myself unwilling to press the trigger.

I lowered the rifle. Maybe Dulles was right. Maybe there comes a point where killing dulls the will and leaves a man open and defenseless. I hoped not. Because if that is true, my days of life were numbered. My name heads up too many lists.

One thing was sure. My hunting days were over.

Such a decision is not unusual, nor is it as sudden as it appears. I know many men who have hunted hard for years and then, perhaps one cold morning on a mountain ridge, have said, "No more."

I took one last look at the buck through my scope, after which I would give a loud whistle and try to scare him up toward Sam.

What I saw, as he turned slightly, froze me. The whistle died on my lips.

The reason the buck had stood in the one spot so long was now obvious. Bright red blood ran down his side and flanks. A long tear along his belly bulged with dark blue intestines. He had been gut-shot, perhaps miles away, and had run this far before his energy gave out. Now he would collapse and, after hours of gasping pain, die.

Unless . . .

I put the cross hairs on his head and squeezed off.

The bullet's impact made a sound like a melon being dropped to a concrete sidewalk. The buck simply vanished from my scope. He had collapsed in a heap, instantly and painlessly dead.

I waded through the snow until I stood over him.

"Sorry, pal," I said. "This just wasn't your day."

His back trail was obvious. Long smudges of blood reddened the crusty snow.

I found myself biting my lip. This deer had been hit hard. He should have had a hunter on his trail.

Slowly, I moved back along his tracks. As I did, I

ejected the spent shell and chambered another. Nothing is sillier than moving into unknown territory with an empty rifle.

I soon discovered that I didn't need another bullet. What I needed was a hearse.

Harry Dassow hung from a branch of a huge maple. Unlike the first three hanged men, he dangled by his feet. His limp fingers trailed in the snow.

His hunting coat and shirt gaped open.

I turned and threw up.

Just like a hung deer, someone had gutted him out.

I backed away, pointed my rifle in the air, and fired off three quick shots.

Sam and I cut him down.

We knew that we shouldn't, but how the hell could we leave him like that?

"Oh, Jesus," Sam mumbled.

"Don't cut the knots," I said. "The boys in the crime lab don't like it when you cut the knots."

All Sam said was, again, "Oh, Jesus."

We left Dassow lying there and climbed down the hill to the jeep, passing the buck I'd put out of his misery. I really should have opened the animal up, to keep the meat from spoiling, but after what we'd seen, I couldn't touch my knife.

It took Sam five minutes to raise another hunting party on the CB radio. He didn't play any games with "Singing Sam" this time. He just started yelling "Emergency!" and clicking his way through the channels, all 23 of them, until he got an answer. The man on the other end relayed his message to somebody in a cabin with a base unit—a bigger, more sophisticated radio that operates on regular electricity instead of batteries. The base station, in turn, contacted the Sheriff's office. Back along the chain of transmissions came Oscar Deep's command: stay right where we were and don't touch anything.

Fair enough. I had touched all I wanted to.

"Harry must have been trailing that buck," Sam said, as we waited. "Ben said he came over the mountain." We were both knocking back the ginger brandy without feeling any of its effects. "Then somebody got him."

"Was he shot?" I asked. "I don't remember seeing a wound."

Sam's face was white. "How the hell could you have, with what they did to him? Jesus, I *hope* they shot him! Can you imagine somebody doing that to you while you were still alive?"

I shrugged. "Either way, he's dead. But why? The first three were outsiders, racketeers. They might have been mixed up in some kind of vendetta. But Dassow was a civilian, straight arrow. Where's the connection?"

"Maybe we've got us a certifiable maniac roaming around, and there isn't any connection."

"A maniac with a hanging fixation? I don't buy that, Sam. Madness is always an easy direction to point. But there's too much damned method to this particular madness. Those first three—hung while they were still

132

alive. Those were tough Syndicate soldiers. Can you see them letting some nut string them up? No, somebody held a cold steady gun on them. As for Dassow, I didn't look too closely, but I don't remember seeing any tracks up there, except for his own and the buck's."

"Somebody else had to be there."

"A lot of that ground is windswept rock without any snow. The hangman could have come in that way. But that's not our problem. There should be tracks, and we'll find them if we make a circle search. My guess, we'll find two more sets."

"Why two?"

"Did you ever try stringing up a two-hundred-pound deadweight by yourself?"

"Once, a big buck down near Sherburne. I didn't get the kinks out of my back for a month."

"Right. It's hard, unless you've got a block and tackle."

Sam took a swig of the brandy and gagged. "Went down the wrong way," he choked.

"You know?" I asked thoughtfully.

"What?" he wheezed.

"Maybe it wasn't the same bunch."

"What?"

"It's just a thought. Maybe somebody hung up Harry as revenge for those first three."

He groaned. "Which means we've got *two* tribes of maniacs roaming around in the woods?"

"Or two groups of very sane professionals with some specific reason for using terror tactics."

133

"That's crazy," he said.

Any further argument was cut off by the arrival of Sheriff Deep's patrol car, followed by a pickup truck filled with blue-uniformed troopers, their faces red from the wind, and their hands hovering near their service revolvers.

The Sheriff piled out of his car, came over to us and jerked his head toward the pickup. "The kid troopers got themselves stuck down the hill. We gave them a lift. Where did the accident take place?"

Sam hadn't gone into detail on the open radio channels, merely reporting an "accidental homicide," if there is such a creature.

Sam said, "I didn't want to come right out on the radio and say what happened. There's been another hanging, Oscar."

The Sheriff studied him carefully. "That's impossible."

"It's Harry Dassow," I said. "Somebody strung him up by his heels and gutted him out like a buck."

Deep leaned toward me. "Don't tell me, Stone. Let me guess. *You* found him, am I right?"

Sam protested, "Warren was only stalking a buck and—"

Deep growled, "Let me hear it from him."

So I told him about the wounded buck, and how I'd backtracked its blood trail.

"Why? You already had your meat and your horns."

"That deer was hit too hard. Somebody *had* to be on his trail."

He spat. "That's all you know. Those lousy road hunters, they'll let a wounded buck get away to die because they're plain too lazy to get out of their car."

"Maybe. Anyway, I backtracked a couple of hundred yards, and that's where I found Dassow."

"Show me."

We had been joined by his deputy, Roy Frisk, who carried a Polaroid camera. He had been driving the pickup.

He told the Sheriff, "Those troopers have been giving me a hard time. They say this is their squawk."

Deep chuckled. "Since they couldn't get up the hill, it ain't, but they're welcome to come along. It'll do my heart good to watch them get those neat lowtop shoes filled with snow."

I led the procession up the hill, past the dead buck. Sheriff Deep scowled at it. "You just going to let that meat lay there and go sour?" he asked.

"I wasn't sure if it might be evidence," I said.

"Okay, I see it. Sam, do you have a knife?"

"Sure."

"Open him up. We'll drag him down to the road on the way back. I hate waste."

I almost laughed. Sam's face was stricken. The last thing he wanted to do on this cold November afternoon was gut out a deer.

The Sheriff prodded my shoulder. "Come on, Stone. We ain't got that much daylight left."

I took the lead again. The Sheriff and his deputy were behind me. Further back, the state troopers cursed

135

their way through the snow.

We stopped a few yards away from the hanging tree.

"You cut him down!" Deep accused.

My patience vanished. "You bet your fat ass I cut him down," I yelled. "You would have, too."

He made a gentle motion with his hand. "Easy, son. I'm not saying I wouldn't have."

Defensively, I said, "I saved the knots."

"Good." To Roy, who was taking pictures, he added, "Don't mess up any tracks."

Roy said, "I don't see any here, except theirs and Harry's. And the buck's."

The troopers arrived, puffing and very wet. Oscar Deep beamed at them. "Which one of you boys brought the body bag?" he asked.

They looked at each other. One, who wore an extra stripe on his sleeve, started to open his mouth. Another trooper, younger, raised his hand and, without a word, started back down toward the road.

Deep sent the rest of them up the hill to flank both sides of the trail made by Dassow and the wounded buck.

When they were out of earshot, Deep said, "You still got that Hartman girl stashed in your motel room?"

"Why?"

"Her friends have been trying to reach her, the ones in Deer Creek. She phoned them for a lift, but when they got to the motel she wasn't around anyplace. Naturally, they didn't know that they might find her in your room."

136

I shook my head. "Not there. I left her in the bar. When I went back, she was gone."

"When was that?"

"About an hour after you dropped me off."

He frowned. "And it's pretty obvious that poor Harry didn't pick her up." He stared down at the still, bloody shape in the snow. "Poor son of a bitch. He had to go and get in the middle."

"Middle? Of what?"

He snapped out of his mood. "Roy, ain't you got those damned pictures done yet?"

"Just now finished, Sheriff."

"All right. Go on up and help those troopers track their way before they get themselves lost." To me, he said, "Let's help Sam drag your deer down to the road."

I hesitated. "Sheriff, I really don't want that deer. I only dropped him because he was already gut-shot."

"You still can't waste him. How about donating him to the prisoners?"

"What prisoners?"

"The ones in the county jail. Fresh meat is always welcome. The money the state gives us to feed them doesn't stretch much further than pork chops once a week."

"Sheriff, you've got yourself some venison," I said.

We beat the troopers back to the road, but not by much. The buck was heavy, and the three of us were sweating when we heaved the carcass into the bed of the pickup truck.

The four troopers were carrying the body bag by its corners. They started to put it into the truck, saw the deer carcass, and hesitated.

One said, "We can't put him in there with that animal."

Patiently, Deep said, "Yes you can. Harry wouldn't mind."

Reluctantly, they arranged the canvas bag alongside the dead buck.

Before Deep could bring it up, I said, "I know. We're supposed to go down to the office and make a statement."

"Right on," said the Sheriff.

Laura took it all down and closed her notebook with a half sob.

"My God," she said. "When is it all going to end?"

"When we find out why it's being done."

Flatly, she told me, "It arrived with you."

"No," I said. "It arrived with that convention of gangsters three years ago. Something started up there in the Dassow mansion that didn't end when the convention broke up."

Deep, who had been listening, said, "Still, son, you've got to admit that trouble seems to follow you around."

"And speaking of trouble, it might be a good idea to put out an All Points on Joan Hartman."

"Oh?" Laura said shortly. "Have you lost little Miss Montana?"

138

"Appears she wandered off," said the Sheriff. "No APB. I'll give it a couple more hours."

"She left her rifle. That doesn't seem right."

"She could have forgot it. You two have a fight?"

"Excuse me," said Laura Jackson. "I've got to type up these statements."

"You know," Sam said, as she left the room, "I didn't think of it at the time—"

"Of what?" I asked.

"When I was driving to the motel this afternoon, Harry's Land Rover passed me, heading south."

"Where?"

"Half a mile or so from the motel."

"It couldn't have been Harry," said the Sheriff. "He was still out in the woods. Maybe dead already."

"And besides, Joan had called her friends for a ride," I said. "Why would she get in the Land Rover?"

"Maybe she didn't have any choice," said the Sheriff. "All right, Stone. You've got your APB. Roy, get out an alert on Miss Hartman, and find out where that Land Rover is and who's driving it."

"Can we go?" I asked.

"You've got to sign those statements."

"Right this very minute?"

He relented. "No. I tell you what, come in anytime today or tomorrow."

"Thanks," I said.

We left.

"Where are we going now?" asked Sam.

"Dassow's place. I want to check it out. Let's move."

He put the jeep in gear and spun the tires on the ice-slick driveway.

We were dirty and tired from poking through the charred ruins.

"I don't know what the hell you expect to find," Sam grumbled.

"Neither do I. But there's *something* up here."

"Maybe there was. And maybe they found it already."

"They? Who, Sam?"

He shrugged. "Whoever's behind all this killing."

"I'm not so sure. This mess reminds me of the way the undercover cells used to be set up. Clandestine groups operating right alongside of each other, none aware of the others' existence. Remember the three we broke up in Rome? All planning to shoot President Johnson when he visited the Vatican, and not one in touch with the other two. This thing has the same smell. I don't think anybody's come up with whatever they're looking for. They're still looking, and still killing each other off."

Sam's voice was tense. "So what? What business is it of ours? Of yours? I thought you didn't work unless you got paid."

"I don't," I said. Then I told him about the nine thousand dollars, and its disappearance.

Positively, he said, "The Hartman girl took it."

"Why?"

"Why does anybody steal? She wanted it."

"I thought so at first, but not now, that I've had time to settle down. Sure, she had the opportunity, but how would she have known it was there?"

"She had plenty of time to search your room, snooping. Maybe she stumbled over it and gave in to temptation."

"I don't read her as a sneak thief."

"Why not? Because she's pretty? Because she comes on like Miss Outdoors? Warren, anybody can make a mistake and grab for a big bundle."

"Sam, you sound like you've been there."

He turned away. "Let's get the hell out of this haunted house."

I followed him toward the jeep. Then I stopped.

"Sam—"

He turned. "What?"

"That patch of weeds near the foundation. Did there use to be a flower garden there?"

"How the hell would I know? Who cares?"

"Get your shovel."

There was a small entrenching tool in the jeep's tool kit. I had seen Sam use it several times to dig the vehicle out of the soft spots in the hills. He grumbled, but he went to fetch it while I squatted down near the patch of vegetation that had caught my eye. It was still brownish green, despite the surrounding snow. I had seen such patches of vegetation before, and I already knew what I would find beneath it. I knew, too, that in the early spring, the plants would bud with bright yellow flowers.

I told Sam, "Something's buried there."

I was right. It was a shallow grave.

Less than three feet down, we found the body.

The years and the worms had done their work on his face, but the man's clothing was still fairly intact, if somewhat rotted. They'd taken his wallet, but in his breast pocket, where I often carry mine when traveling, was a B.P. gasoline credit card and, stamped on its indestructible plastic, the name "Vincent Hartman."

"Jesus!" said Sam. "We can't turn up at the Sheriff's office with another body! Oscar wouldn't have any choice but to lock us up and throw away the key!"

"We're not reporting this one," I said. "Let's cover him up again."

I had slipped the credit card into my own pocket without Sam's seeing it. We did the best job of disguising our excavation, smoothing the earth down and throwing some nearby charred wallboard over the spot. A gentle snow had begun to fall, and it would soon eliminate any signs that remained of our presence.

As we drove down the hill, Sam said, "That guy's been there all this time?"

"Three years."

We had both seen the jagged hole left in the bleaching skull by an expanding bullet. A typical gangland execution.

142

"Why would they have left him there?" Sam asked.

"Why not? Who expected somebody like us to come snooping around a private mansion, especially one that had burned down? In another few years, the forest would have taken it all back, foundations and every-thing, including our underground friend."

Sam bit his lip. "This whole thing seems to be getting out of hand."

I didn't answer. Sam had something worrying at him. Maybe he would tell me, maybe he wouldn't. But no amount of prodding would hasten the process.

When he turned onto the hard road, he said, "Why don't we just go on to my place? Jenny's expecting you."

"Who did she fix me up with tonight?"

He managed a chuckle. "Nobody. I told you it was family. But don't think she didn't have her Christmas list out. I finally convinced her that you've already got more action than you can handle."

"Thanks. Stop by the motel and let me change."

"Not to worry. Jenny doesn't care."

"Speak for yourself, Superman. My ass is wet. And I smell like a polar bear."

"Oh, all right. Not to—"

"Sam?"

"What?"

"Please, unless you want to drive me right up a tree, please don't say 'not to worry' any more."

He gave me a surprised look, almost said, "Not to worry," didn't, and we drove in silence for a while.

Then: "I heard it in a Richard Burton movie. I always thought I sort of sounded like him."

"Only when you say 'not to worry.' At other times, you sound like Greta Garbo."

He mumbled something impolite, and mashed the gas pedal to the floor.

13

Somebody had presented me with a Sony cassette recorder. It waited for me on top of the TV set. I felt like Alice in Wonderland. All that was missing was a note saying, PLAY ME.

But I figured it out anyway. I pressed the PLAY button.

A man's voice said, "Mr. Stone, we're fed up with you. We made you a fair offer, and you put one of us on crutches."

In his pause, I yelled back, "Yeah, you son of a bitch, and you stole my nine thousand dollars!"

As if he had heard me, the taped voice said, "So we come and took back our money. Now we've got another offer." A second pause. "Talk, damn it!"

Joan Hartman's voice said, "Warren, tell them to take

145

a flying jump!" There came a scuffling noise, and a choked scream. The man's voice said, "In case you didn't recognize Miss Loudmouth, she's Joan Hartman, and if you don't want to find her in a ditch, you'd better get your gear and get the hell out of the state by tomorrow morning. If you do, we'll let her go. If you don't think we mean business, you might check out the north slope of Garnett Hill."

The sound track ended. I almost expected a voice to say,"This tape will self-destruct in five seconds."

"What's Garnett Hill?" I asked.

Softly, Sam said, "That's where we found Harry Dassow."

I rewound the cassette, and then pressed the PLAY button again.

All we heard this time was a hissing noise.

I swore. The oldest dodge in the electronics world, and I'd fallen for it. I popped out the cassette and checked the tape path. Sure. They'd wired in an extra erase head, just a small chunk of permanent magnet, right after the playback head. So, just a fraction of a second after we'd heard the tape, it was erasing itself. Somebody was being very careful about voice print identification.

"Come on," I told Sam. "Help me get packed."

He stared. "You're letting them run you? How do you know they'll let her go anyway?"

"I don't. But I damned well know what they'll do if I *don't* run."

"They might have killed her five minutes after they made that tape."

"They probably did," I said, feeling the sour taste rising up inside my throat. "If I was operating in their place, I would have."

Dinner was a barrel of fun.

My old Dodge van was parked outside, with all my gear cluttering its rear compartment. Jenny Keith had sensed our low spirits when we came in, and set about reinforcing us with a brace of vicious martinis. They warded off absolute collapse, but nothing could have cheered us up.

I love spaghetti, and Jenny has a knack with the red sauce that will eventually win her the Italian Medal of Honor. It was wasted on me tonight.

She didn't ask a single question. She seemed to be everywhere, serving food, pouring wine, passing the cheese, topping off the espresso. Mrs. Perfect.

So, why was it, half an hour later when we were seated before the fire, that we were spilling our guts to her?

When we had finished our confessions, she asked me, "And you're going home?"

"That's it."

She sipped her brandy, shook her head. "No."

"No what, Jenny?"

"No, I don't believe you. Not one word."

"I don't have much choice. They'll kill her. They've

147

already shown us how serious they are."

"The Warren Stone I know would say, 'She's just got to take her own chances,' and then move mountains to rescue her."

"Which might only result in both of us getting killed. Running's easier."

"You're still lying."

I looked down at the flickering fire. What right did it have to be so colorful and cheerful? I tossed what was left of my brandy into the flames, and they flared with a bright blue light for a moment.

"Okay," I said. "I admit it. I'm tired of going down this road anyway. It's not the girl. It's what I'm afraid I'm going to find."

"What? Or who?"

"Do I have to say the name?"

"Yes, Warren. You have to."

I leaned back and looked at Sam Keith. "What about it, buddy? After all these years, are you going to force me to put it into words?"

He had seemed to shrink into himself in the last few moments. Slowly, he shook his head.

"No. Jenny . . . Warren is afraid he'll find me down at the end of that road."

Calmly, as if it had no importance, she asked, "And will he?"

His voice trembled as he said, "Yes."

"Excuse me," said his wife. She got up and left the room.

Sam asked, "How long have you suspected?"

"Not long. But the things you said . . . the way you acted. They jarred me. I tried not to notice. I didn't want to. But this afternoon—"

"Me and my big mouth. Warren—it was only money. None of this . . . violence. I swear."

I shrugged. "But whatever it was that you did, it set off these killings. Didn't it?"

"I'm afraid so. I didn't mean to, but—"

He gulped the rest of his drink. Jenny returned.

"Here," she said. "I was going to tear this up, but now I'm glad I saved it."

She handed me a letter typed on official General Administration stationery.

It was addressed to Sam, and the message was brief. It had been decided that his injury was not service-connected, since the hijack operation in which he'd been injured was not officially approved. His pension was canceled, and they wanted repayment of some forty-three thousand dollars which he had collected already.

"Those bastards!" I said. "Excuse me, Jenny."

"Never mind. I said worse."

"When did you get this, Sam?"

"More than a year ago." He stared at the letter. "Closer to two years, I guess." It was as if the letter had just arrived, the way he looked at it. "Since then, they've hit me with a lawsuit and tried to seize the house and land."

"Don't you have a lawyer?"

"A good one. He's been holding them off. But . . .

149

well, we both learned it the hard way, Warren. You can't beat City Hall."

"No, but you can blow it up."

Bitterly, Jenny said, "That's what you went and did, isn't it, Warren?" Her tone surprised me.

"In a way," I said. "I found out they'd been using me like some kind of robot. I couldn't take that."

"So you lit the torch. The only thing is, my dear, that poor Sam got caught in the fallout." She slapped the letter. "That's why they did this to him. Because the two of you were so close, don't you see? It was a way of getting back at you."

"Yes," I nodded. What a lousy waste it had all been. None of us had emerged unscathed. Not me, not poor Alice, not even my friends. And Sam was right, you couldn't beat them. As fast as you cut one head off the Hydra, another two grew back.

I asked, "What have you been living on?"

Sam looked up at Jenny. She gave him a slight smile. "Go on, Sam. I haven't been prying, but not even I am stupid enough to believe we've been making it on what you take in at the gun shop."

He got up and, slowly, poured us all hefty brandies.

"It all started three years ago," he said, "when that bunch got together up at Judge Dassow's place."

It had been the first mass convocation of organized crime since the early sixties, when an earlier group of criminal overlords had consorted with a handful of Washington officials in planning the Dallas assassination

150

of John Fitzgerald Kennedy. That operation had gone off without a hitch, and relatively cheaply, with each of the seven regional families contributing ten million dollars.

I'd heard rumors of the Agency being involved in Kennedy's murder. "Where did you get this?"

"I heard it up at the mansion," he said.

This time, the target had been several men, and the job was more dangerous because government protection was lacking.

Nine officials were to be hit, including the Secretary of Transportation, his aides, and two key supervisors of Amtrack. Improved rail service had been cutting into interstate trucking profits, resulting in lowered payments from the trucking industry to the Syndicate accounts. So the decision had been made to put the railroads out of business—or, at least, back to where they had languished in the early seventies.

Sam had noticed the activities at the mansion weeks before the law took interest.

"I knew right away it was big," he said. "So I planted a couple of bugs. It wasn't hard. Those were city boys. They had the road covered like a blanket, but I came through the woods."

"Why? You were a civilian. What was in it for you?"

"Nothing, at least not then. I was itchy. You know whatit's like, not having anything to do. I guess I was looking for an edge. I wouldn't have tied in with them, anything like that. But maybe there was something else. Listen, Warren, even when the pension was coming in, we weren't exactly rolling in money. Maybe if I'd known from the beginning how big the operation was, I'd have stayed away. But for all I knew, it was just a meeting to cut up territories, or establish new routes for shipping drugs."

I didn't say anything.

His bugs had picked up their planning against the railroads, and the Washington officials, threats made more real by what he overheard about the Kennedy assassination.

"That's when I dropped a blind tip to Oscar Deep," Sam said. "He never knew it came from me. Him and Ben started bird-dogging them, and the next thing, the feds were in the act, and then the whole thing blew apart." He took a deep breath. "Except, from what I'd heard, I knew they had brought a war chest along to finance the railroad operation. And they didn't take it out, because everybody was being searched, right down to their underwear."

"So they stashed it up there, and you found it."

"Right and wrong. They'd stashed it, all right. I thought I knew where. But somebody beat me to it."

"Vince Hartman?"

"Right. And I guess they got him soon after, and that's how he ended up in that hole."

"Are you sure?"

"Why else would they have killed him?"

"I don't know." I tapped the pension cancellation. "You must have found something."

"Seed money, that's all. Fifty thousand in small bills.

152

It was shoved up in one of the false ceilings. I tore that place apart, but I never found another dime."

"Maybe there wasn't any more."

"Warren, they had at least twenty million. Probably more. My guess is, Vince hid it somewhere."

"If so, why did they kill him before they found it?"

"Maybe they forced him to tell, then—"

"No. They're still looking for it. That's why we're up to our hips in gangsters. They haven't given up, and they aren't going to." I finished my brandy. "I'm sorry my troubles with the Agency rubbed off on you. But now you've paid me back, with interest. The mob thinks I'm on the job against them, and they're after me. They even threatened Alice. That's why I shot that bastard this morning. But nobody suspects Sam Keith, good old Sam, local gunsmith. I'm the big noise in town, and would you please tell me how the hell I get them to believe that I'm just an innocent bystander who only wanted to go deer hunting?"

"I'm sorry, Warren. I didn't know it would turn out like this."

"No, you didn't. But if I had known about your fifty-thousand-dollar caper, I might have handled things differently. Now I'm boxed in. They've got that girl, they've got their sights set square on my head. I don't have room to stretch."

Jenny spoke. "But will running really help?"

I considered. "An hour ago, I thought so. Now, I don't think it will. This mess isn't going to dry up and blow away. Sam, when you retired, did you turn in your

153

brains along with your poison needle? Haven't you figured out, yet, that there's another force involved here, one beyond the Syndicate? You don't think they strung up their own men, do you?"

"Depends. They killed Vince Hartman."

"Did they?"

He didn't answer.

I drove down the windswept highway to Utica, checked into the Quality Motel, unloaded the van, rented a Toyota from an outfit that claimed to be "Number 3, and trying even harder."

With my rifle and gear in the Toyota's trunk, I drove right back up Route 28 to Old Forge, where I found an out-of-the-way hotel that didn't even have a lighted sign outside. To be exact, it was an Inn, as in Ye Olde.

I sat in the dark quietness of my room, thinking.

All right. The Dassow mansion was Ground Zero. Everything radiated out from there.

And buried under Ground Zero was Joan Hartman's father, Vince. He was known as the best enforcer in the business. How had he gotten stupid enough to let somebody blow out his brains?

It had to be someone he trusted. But who? Hartman wouldn't have trusted his own brother.

Then the answer spread itself out before me, and I realized what I had to do.

I wasn't really trying to stay under cover. My departure from the motel might fool them for a few hours, but when I didn't turn up at check points down south, particularly at Louisville late tomorrow, the game would be over. That would be when they'd become sure that I had chosen sides against them.

Would they turn Joan loose before then?

I doubted it. I wouldn't have.

They were softer than me.

They did. A motorist found her, blindfolded and hands tied behind her back, wandering down the side of the highway.

By then, I was back in contact with Sam Keith. He had lent me one of his CB radios, and I was broadcasting, unlicensed, as Blue Racer. His new handle was Greta Garbo, which brought us a few blue comments from passing truck drivers.

Joan had been taken to the Sheriff's office in Bear Paw. It took a while for Sam to get this information over to me, since we were talking in an improvised code, in which she was the Little Brown Jug, and the Sheriff had become the Deep Blue Sea. The code wouldn't have fooled any serious listener, but we kept switching channels, and the chances were good that nobody who counted would overhear us.

I told him to take her to his place. It was risky for me to meet there, but riskier still for him to come to me.

With the Toyota parked a couple of long blocks from his house, I cut through icy back yards to his rear porch.

Jenny let me in. She had been crying.

Sam hadn't gotten back yet. We had coffee. "I'm

155

sorry," Jenny told me. "It just hit me. After I waited all that time for Sam to get free of that cowboy and Indian game you were all playing, he's right back in the middle of it."

I didn't want to be harsh. But I had to say, "He volunteered this time, Jenny. Somehow, we could have gotten his pension back for him. Instead, he went for the easy money. I guess he forgot that it's never easy."

She touched my hands. "Don't hate him, Warren, please. He respects you so much."

"Jenny, I don't hate him. It's just that I'm disappointed in him. And afraid for him. He's not fast enough any more." She started to protest, and I said, "Oh, I don't mean his leg. Mentally. Listen, you don't go up against the big boys part time. You have to work and train like an athlete, or you'll get rolled over."

"Warren! You won't let him get hurt!"

I leaned over and kissed her cheek. "Not on your chinny chin chin, little girl."

She laughed gently. "You're cute. Maybe I waited all that time for the wrong one."

"No. You got the good one. Besides, I already had somebody waiting too."

She sobered. "Yes, you did." She poured me some more coffee. "Does it hurt you to talk about her?"

"Not any more."

"How did it happen?"

"Stupidly. She had to do her own thing."

"What does that mean? Warren, you ought to hear the hostility in your voice!"

"I hear it. I mean it. It wasn't enough for her to be a terrific looker, and great in bed, and fun out of it, and the best cook this side of Paris. Hell, no. She had to fulfill herself too. It took her a long time to find something that I couldn't do, so I couldn't compete with her, but finally she came up with it."

Trying to joke, Jenny said, "I thought you could do everything."

"Wrong. I can't go into a phone booth and shut the door. I can't crawl under a car. I can't even ride in an elevator without sweating."

"Claustrophobia?"

"The worst. And, as Alice happily discovered, that meant that I couldn't crawl down a cave with her spelunking buddies. In case I didn't mention it, we've got one hell of a lot of caves in Kentucky."

"I know."

"Well, as spelunkers go, she was good at it. And all I could do was wait topside, holding her lunch box. She got a big kick out of that, crawling out all covered with red mud and laughing about almost getting caught under a rockfall. I should have kicked her ass all the way over the Rough River!"

"Warren, I'm sorry. You don't have to tell it all."

"Hell, kid, I'm not even started yet."

"Come on, let's go in by the fire."

"No, not now."

"Warren, I'm going—"

I caught her wrist. "No, you're not. You wanted to hear. Now you will."

She squeezed my fingers until they ached. "Don't, Warren. I'm sorry. I was just hurt and angry about Sam. Don't hurt yourself."

"Don't worry, Jenny. It's a good hurt. Like squeezing a boil. It smarts like hell for a couple of minutes, but it lets the pressure out, and you feel better afterwards."

Alice and her friends had gone down into a branch of Horse Cave. Most of the well-known caverns, some under state and federal park authority, are no more dangerous than strolling through a city playground. In fact, considering what's been happening in our cities recently, maybe even safer.

But this branch, which was entered through a low crawlway halfway up a rocky slope, had not been mapped out by anyone but local climbers.

I remember telling Alice, "You're nuts. I've only been back from Germany two days, and you want to celebrate by crawling down into a hole in the ground?"

She kissed me—little nibbling pinches of her lips, promising much but delivering nothing. "I'm sorry, baby. But I didn't know you'd show up, and this has been set up for weeks. I can't let the others down. It'll only take a couple of hours."

She was wrong. What it took was the rest of her life.

I was waiting near the crawlway, sipping a can of Bud, when they came bursting out. Three of them. But four had gone down.

Two were slim young men, covered with yellow mud, and gasping for breath. The third was a hefty girl

158

with stringy brown hair.

My Alice is slim, and has short blonde hair.

I grabbed one of the men. "What happened?"

He gasped, "Gas!"

"Where's Alice?"

Making vague motions toward the cave, he choked, "In a pocket. She was leading. By the time we realized what had happened, we were all hit by it."

My grip tightened. "Why didn't you pull her out? Weren't you roped?"

"It broke. I couldn't help it, Mr. Stone. We did our best."

I slammed him against the rock outcropping. "Your best, hell! Where is she? Why did you come out without her?"

"We need oxygen. I'm going down to the ranger station—"

"You're going nowhere. She'd be dead before you got there."

The other young man said, "Listen, you can't make us go back down there."

I realized he was right. Oh, I could force them to go inside, but once they were out of my sight, they could just hole up without risking the gas again.

The thought of sliding down inside the dark earth made me gag on my own spit. But there wasn't any other choice.

I shoved my man toward the hole. "Let's go. You take the lead."

"We can't—"

"Get the hell in there!"

The other two started to protest, but I had my man in a tight come-along grip, and he was in enough pain to go without resistance. It was cold, but I felt the sweat pop out on my face. It dripped down my sides, too.

I kept pushing him until he was well inside the crawlway. Then I had to let him go, because my hands were shaking so hard.

"Mr. Stone," he protested, "you don't have any right to—"

Maybe I couldn't hold him, but I could reach out and give him a pinch on the nerve complex in his neck that made him yelp with pain.

"Listen," I said, my voice hoarse with anger and my own fear, "you went down this rat hole with my wife, and you came out without her. Now you're going back to get her, and I'm going along to be sure you do."

With the air of somebody holding four aces, he said, "Alice told me about you. You can't take it. You won't get down fifty yards."

"Let's try it, sonny. Move your ass. And hear this. Either we come out of here with her, or you won't be coming out at all."

"I'll report you."

"Report anything you want. Once we get her out."

He wanted to argue some more, but I gave him another little pinch, and he converted his protest into a little groan. Slowly, he started working his way along the passage.

I don't know how long it took us. The walls were closing in on me. My brain swam inside a skull that tried to compress it to the size of a jelly bean. If the man ahead had only known it, he could have subdued me with a hard look.

He must have called something back to me at least twice before I answered, "Huh?"

"She's down there. Past that rockfall. We heard her coughing. I was second on the line. We were all getting dizzy. I tried to pull her up with the rope, but it was old and broke."

"So you just left her there."

He was almost weeping with fear and frustration. "Mr. Stone, you just don't understand. That gas is deadly. You can't smell it. We were lucky to get out ourselves."

"So that crap about going down to the ranger station for oxygen was just so much smoke."

"We'll still need it to recover her—"

He didn't have to say "body."

The passage was high enough for both of us to stand, so I got up close to him.

"All right," I said. "Now, we're both going down there fast, and we'll grab her and get the hell back up here. Maybe we can hold our breaths all the way, maybe not."

"We'll never make it."

"We're sure in hell going to try. If we get out, I'll shut up about the way you ran out on her."

161

"But what if we don't get out?"

I told him, "Well, it won't make any difference then, will it?"

Jenny was crying.

"But, Warren. You got her out alive. You saved her, the two of you."

"We saved her body," I said. "But her brain was oxygen-starved too long. The machines are keeping something alive, but it isn't her. My Alice is still trapped down there in that underground hole."

14

Sam arrived with Joan Hartman, and for a while everything was a flurry of drinks being poured, and that was fine, because I had squeezed the boil enough and felt cleansed.

Bluntly, I told Joan, "They used you as bait to chase me out of town."

"I know. I overheard them talking."

"They aren't very tough. If it had been me, I would have held onto you until Warren Stone was positively seen back in Kentucky."

"They wanted to. Or worse. But something happened. Somebody else arrived. And he was mad as hell with them for the way things had been handled. By then, I had managed to get my feet untied, and one of the original ones caught me. He wanted to shoot me on the spot."

"Which one? Fred or Charlie?"

"Fred. The one who came into the motel bar and said that Harry had sent him to pick me up. I started to tell him that I'd just made arrangements for a ride, but he showed me a little automatic hidden under his coat, so I went along. When I got in the front seat of the Land Rover, somebody stuck a blindfold over my eyes."

"Which one did you see?"

"Fred."

"Did he have a bandage on his leg?"

"No."

Then it had been Charlie I'd shot. I wished now that I had aimed higher.

"What did the new man say, the one who was mad at them?"

"They called him Vito. He tore their hides off and reminded them that Vince Hartman was my father. He asked me to promise to keep quiet about anything I'd heard. I told him that I hadn't heard anything worth repeating, but that if I did, I'd broadcast it to the world to pay them back for what they did to my father."

"What did Vito have to say to that?"

"He swore on his mother's grave that nobody in the Syndicate had anything to do with my father's disappearance. He said they were looking for him too."

"How did he explain them telling you about him being overseas, and how they ripped off your mother?"

"He didn't bring it up, and I didn't ask."

I sighed and put my drink down. "You were lucky. Unless—"

164

She waited. Finally, she asked, "Unless what?"

"Unless they had a change of heart and decided that instead of a Warren Stone back in Kentucky, they'd rather have one up here underground."

Sam said, "They didn't follow us back here, I made sure of that."

I shook my head sadly. "Times have changed, Sam. This isn't Berlin, and we're not in a safehouse. For God's sake, you're even in the phone book. How much brains does it take for them to work their way through Joan's options? Where can she go? To her friends in Deer Creek? Back home to Montana? Or, maybe along with one of my friends, to me?"

Sam bit his lip. "So this place may already be staked out."

"*If* they don't really believe I ran."

"They don't," Joan said. "At least, Vito doesn't. He really laid into them about the way they'd pressured you."

"What did he say?"

"That the only way to handle a man like Warren Stone is to kill him, or—"

"Or what?"

She didn't like saying it. "Or buy him off."

"Well," I said, smiling tightly, "I guess we'll find out which way Vito decided before too much longer.

I always drive back roads as if I knew them, which I don't. But in upper New York State, which laid out its roads on the grid system, it is possible to be unsure of

165

where you are, yet not be lost seriously because eventually you will always come out on a road that you recognize.

One thing this method of driving accomplishes is to make it easy to tell if somebody's following you. Somebody was.

"I'm sorry," I told Joan Hartman.

"Why? You're helping me."

"No I'm not. I'm helping me. I'm using you as bait."

She gave a little laugh. "Why not? At least that might accomplish something. All I seem to be doing is kicking shi . . . snow."

The car following us lay well back, running without lights. That was possible, the way the moon was reflecting off the snow.

"We've got three choices," I said. "Outrun them, outguess them, or—"

"Or stop and see what they want."

"You named it."

"What are you going to do?"

"Stop."

"Why?"

"Maybe I'd like them to buy me out. I can use the money."

"What if they intend the—other?"

"That'd take some doing on their part. It's been tried by experts."

"So I've heard."

"I'm going to take that next hill fast, switch off my lights and make a U-turn. You might jump out and hide

166

in the apple trees. When things calm down, walk down to the main road. You can see the lights down there, maybe half a mile. It'll take you ten minutes. I'll keep them busy longer than that."

"How?"

"I'm going to block the road near the hill's crest. Once they stop, they'll never get enough traction on this ice to go on up again. They won't be able to knock even a little Toyota out of the way."

She didn't bother to consider the choice I'd given her. "No way, my friend. I don't like walking home from a date."

"Okay," I said. "Hang on."

As I topped the hill, when my lights would normally vanish from the following driver's view, I switched them off and threw the Toyota into a controlled skid. It's a tricky business, involving equal jockeying of the brake and throttle, but the result was that I turned around in the road and drifted to a stop. I eased on the gas and crept back to the top of the hill where I turned the car broadside across the narrow road.

When, by the sound, I figured they were fifty yards or so down the hill, I flashed on my lights which reflected off the snowbanks and lit up the area like a flare. Their driver revved his engine, and his tires whined furiously against the ice. I heard a grinding of gears, and their car began sliding back down the hill.

I leaned over the top of the Toyota. "Cut your wheels!" I yelled.

The driver did, and his rear wheel lurched into the

left-hand ditch. His engine stalled and died.

"Be careful," Joan said, crouching down behind the door.

"They want to talk," I said. "Otherwise, they could have taken us half a dozen times already. I made it easy for them."

She said something. I didn't catch it all, but what I did wasn't very ladylike.

From down the road, a voice called, "Is that you, Stone?"

I shouted back, "No! You've been following a Pizza Hut delivery!"

"We want to talk."

"All right. Talk."

"Not like this. Can we come up there?"

"How many of you?"

"Two."

"No. I'll come down."

Joan grabbed my arm. "Don't do it!"

"Take my advice, kid," I said. "Hike down to that main road and catch yourself a bus back to Montana."

"Not until I find out what happened to my father."

I knew damned well what had happened to her father, but up to now I hadn't found the way to break it to her. And certainly now wasn't the time to do it.

"Okay," I said. "Stay here. But if you hear shooting or yelling, you run like hell."

"No."

I swore under my breath, and handed her my .357 Magnum. "To fire this thing," I said, "all you have to do

168

is point it and squeeze the trigger. It shoots six times."

She took it. I added, "Please don't try any rescue operations. I sure in hell don't want to be hit by my own bullets. Especially *these* bullets. Don't use it unless they come up here after you."

"We'll see," she said.

I zipped up my hunting coat and half walked, half slid, down to the ditched car. When I got close, they turned on their lights and blinded me. I moved off to one side, out of the direct beams, and reached their left front door.

"Hello, Warren," said Laura Jackson. "Surprise."

15

The man in the front seat with Laura introduced himself as Vito Sinatra. I gave a laugh, and he said, "So help me, it's true!"

"Okay," I said. "But Old Blue Eyes isn't going to like it when he finds out."

Laura said, "Very cute and very clever. That's the impression you've left in your wake, Warren. Cute and clever. But not too smart."

"Can I get in?" I asked. "I'm freezing."

"Up here," she said. She twisted her body over the seat and ended up sitting in the back. I crawled in and felt the warmth she'd left against the plastic cushions. I hate them. Easy to keep clean, but the sweat sticks to your back in the summer and in winter, you need an electric blanket to keep your spine from turning to ice cubes.

"I was expecting you, Vito," I said. "But not your lady friend."

He said, "Miss Jackson is what you might call our local correspondent."

"My, my," I said. "And here all this time I thought she was only a lady lawyer."

"Get to it, Vito," she said harshly.

He didn't raise his voice to her. The results were instant, anyway.

"In time. Meanwhile, perhaps you might shut that lovely mouth?"

To me, he added, "Flag of truce? No tricks from either one of us?"

"That's fine with me."

I didn't mean it any more than he did. But it set a nice tone.

He nudged me a little. "I presume you didn't leave Miss Hartman unarmed?"

"She's carrying," I admitted. "But I told her not to use it unless you decided to go wandering up in her direction."

"Then, not to worry," said Laura. The little whiff of chocolate came from her again. I wondered why she didn't have the interior of that Chevy dry-cleaned. "Vito, you will learn that when Warren Stone speaks, the weaker sex listens."

Without turning, Vito Sinatra said, "I already warned you."

Laura made a rude noise in her throat, but she didn't add anything to it.

I told Vito, "Just leave Miss Hartman alone, and things will be quiet. Nobody's looking to start a war."

"Fine," he said. "Perhaps you'd like a little wine?"

I laughed. "Maybe you *are* a Sinatra. You're stuck in an icy ditch in the middle of the night on a snowbound mountain, and you offer me wine? Well, I accept."

"Forgive the bottle," he said, handing me an already-opened jug of Chianti. It was nicely chilled by the night air. I made a little toasting gesture and sipped from its neck.

"Thanks."

He took some himself, politely not wiping the bottle, and offered it to Laura.

She made an "Ecch" sound.

"It seems you've upset Miss Jackson," he said.

"Lovers' spat," I said.

Chuckling, he said, "I see."

"Oh, damn you both!" she shrilled from the back seat.

"Mr. Stone," he said with composure, "I am a businessman. I'm interested in the highest profit for the least risk. I carry no vendetta, indulge in no revenge. Unless it is profitable."

"A noble attitude," I said. "I try to follow those rules myself."

"So I understand. We have heard of you. In West Virginia, in Kansas, in Ohio. And, particularly, in Nevada."

"Yeah," I said. "I didn't intend it, but Nevada got kind of noisy."

"It might have been noisier," he said. "But we took

a hand there. Didn't you ever wonder why, when it appeared you would expose the mayor of Henderson to national shame, that he decided to become permanently dead?"

"Not really," I said. "He had the heart of a rabbit. And they called it suicide."

Vito chuckled. "You're right, he was a rabbit. He feared death so much that he had already invested more than a hundred thousand dollars in a plan to be frozen on the occasion of his death and preserved for years, perhaps centuries, against the chance that a cure for whatever killed him might be discovered. But no one will ever discover a cure for a forty-five caliber bullet. I might add that the money he wasted was skimmed from several of our casino money rooms."

"I see the light," I said. "Well, I didn't have anything against the man, but the good guys in his town did, and they put up twenty-five thousand bucks for me to bring him down. Why didn't you just wait and let me do it? I had enough on him to send him up for fifty years."

"We felt the publicity was unwise," said Vito Sinatra.

"That figures."

He told me, "Your reputation is good. You realize that there is no conscience printed on a dollar bill. Yet you have limits of conscience in what you will do to earn it."

"You're breaking my heart," I said. "I came down here because I thought you had a deal to offer, and it turns out I'm being nominated for sainthood."

He bellowed with laughter and took a hearty swig of

the wine before passing the bottle. "You should be with us," he said. "We admire heart."

"I admire money," I said. "Make your offer. I've got heavy gambling debts."

"No," he objected. "You do not gamble. At least with money. And you need three thousand dollars a month, thirty-six thousand dollars a year to keep your wife alive on those machines. And you pray that one day there will be a reversal, that her dead brain may miraculously come to life again."

"Wrong," I said. "I gave up on miracles a long time ago."

Softly, he said, "Then why not pull the plug?"

I poured down maybe half a cup of wine and choked. "Would you, Vito?"

"Me? Not in a thousand years! Not while there is still hope."

"But there is no hope. That's what I'm trying to tell you."

"No, you are not." He shared the wine. "Oh, your head tells you there is no hope, but who believes his head? Your heart knows what is best."

There came a strange sound from the back seat. It was Laura. She was uttering a strange mixture of laughter and sobbing. She leaned forward and caught my head—actually, both my ears—in her hands and turned me around so hard that I was afraid she would break my neck.

"Warren, you poor son of a bitch!" she said caressingly. "Oh, you poor son of a bitch."

174

"Same to you, lady," I mumbled.

"Please," said Vito.

"In a minute," Laura said. She leaned forward and kissed me hard. "I forgive you. Go on, make it with the lady from Montana. You and me, we were only a one-night stand."

"Business!" said Vito crisply. "Mr. Stone, it's my opinion that you came here merely for a deer hunt, as you claim."

"It's too bad Fred and Charlie didn't take my word for that," I said.

"Did you really have to shoot Charlie?"

"Is that his real name?"

"No. Try Chauncey."

I choked. "Chauncey? I thought all of you guys were from Italy."

"We accept minority groups. Even Irish. I'm sorry about what Chauncey did. I understand he threatened your wife. That was wrong. We do not reach at a man through his family. It's one of the oldest rules."

"But a rule they're bending these days, right? Remember Yablonski's wife and daughter? Shot dead, along with him."

"True," he agreed. "But such things do not happen in *my* organization. Those killers, they were union hotheads."

"Okay," I said. "Apology accepted."

"My original offer still holds," he said. "Nine thousand dollars for leaving a deer hunt that obviously holds no real interest for you anyway."

"It's too late," I said. "I didn't mind finding those three boys of yours strung up in the trees. But since then, I've been searched. I've been hassled. I've been shot at."

"Only in warning. Fred is more stable than Chauncey. He was careful that nobody would be hurt."

"Unless his hand shook."

"Accidents happen," he shrugged. "But there's no blame in that case. We took all deliberate care."

I asked, "Do you know who you sound like?"

"Who?"

"A tricky lawyer who used to work for a trickier President named Nixon."

He laughed. "Your file shows that you have an unfriendly attitude toward the national government."

"I don't like people who manipulate other people. I spent years as a puppet without knowing it. I thought the good guys were pulling my strings. Then I found out that there aren't any good guys."

"Mr. Stone, you are very cynical."

"Hell, call me Warren. After all, we're drinking out of the same bottle."

Laura put in, "Warren, don't forget that I was in that car too. I'd told them I'd be driving you home. But I didn't know they were going to shoot at us."

"I believe you. You couldn't have faked your reactions. Unless you happen to be a better actress than Faye Dunaway."

She said, "I don't think Faye Dunaway is a very good actress."

176

"That's what I mean."

Vito said, "What are your other complaints?"

"I won't go into the little matter of my room being searched. Or my nine thousand dollars being swiped."

He said, "It was *our* nine thousand. You hadn't accepted our offer."

"Maybe I was going to. You didn't give me the chance."

"Perhaps. What else?"

"Where things got a little sick-making was finding Harry Dassow strung up like a dressed-out deer. That was a little hard to take."

"I agree. An unfortunate excess of zeal."

"By *your* boys?"

"Yes. But against specific orders."

"Goody. What are you going to do, slap their wrists?"

His voice would have cut glass. "Mr. Stone . . . Warren . . . those two fools are going to be very unhappy for a long time. If it weren't for past services, they would be underground right now."

"Underground? That reminds me of another discovery that bothered me."

"What else can there be?"

"The matter of Vince Hartman."

"What about him?"

"I found him. Underground. Under about three feet of it. Whoever planted him didn't even take the time to do a good job of it."

He lifted the bottle and it was empty. He tossed it out

of the window. Another charge against Vito. Littering the trail.

His voice came low and muffled. "We don't know anything about Vince Hartman. We've been looking for that bastard for three years."

"Well, I can take you right to him. And my guess is he's been underground there all the time you've been looking."

"This is disturbing news," he said. "Very well. Warren, I think we can improve on our original offer."

"Really? Why?"

"Because it seems you can be of more benefit to us by your presence than your absence."

"In other words, instead of running me off, now you want to employ my special services?"

"Yes, I think so."

"It'll be more expensive than you think."

"Why? Do you hold a grudge?"

"You bet your bippy I hold a grudge!" As I said it, I had a flash of the B.P. credit card I had found on the body of Joan's father, and I gave a reluctant nod toward the pun-making ability of the subconscious. "Vito, you and your boys tried to *run* me. And I pretended to run."

He admitted, "We thought you *had* run. You have the reputation of being a sensible man. There's nothing of value for you here. Why should you risk your life?"

"Nothing of value except my pride. And that's what's going to cost you. Because, Vito, without my pride, I'm dead. It's all that keeps me alive."

From the back seat, Laura Jackson murmured, "And it keeps your wife alive, too. Sucker."

Vito almost snarled, "Shut your face! This man—"

"Hush, hush, sweet Vito. I'm making him a compliment. We burnt-out cases make fun of men like him, but believe me, if the bad thing ever happens to us, it's suckers like Warren Stone we want at our sides."

I sniffed the air. "Give," I said.

"What—?"

"You've got a bottle stashed back there. Share the wealth."

She passed up what was left of a pint of Black Velvet. Maybe half a bottle.

"Thanks, baby. I knew something was up. You were getting too nice to me." I sipped, and passed the bottle to Vito Sinatra.

Poor Joan. Freezing up there with only my .357 Magnum as companionship. I had an urge to call her down to our relative warmth, and realized that I had to watch myself, that I was beginning to feel the booze even though I'd drunk far less than I could normally handle. "What I mean, Vito, is that once I've been put on the run, I have to pay back. Don't you understand? If I didn't pay back, I'd never trust myself again. You know what I mean."

"Yes," he said. "Very well. You must believe me, however. We did not kill Vincent Hartman. I want you to find us the one who did, and—"

"No," I said. "That's not what you want."

"Oh?"

"You want what Vince hijacked from you. How much was it? Around ten million? Not as much as fifteen, because that's all you paid for the JFK hit."

"Eleven million, more or less," he said.

I had a mental flash of the fifty thousand that Sam had taken care of on the "less" side.

"Small bills," he added. "And the hell of it is, all laundered. Not a hot serial number in the whole batch. That adds another two million street value to it."

"Suppose I do find it. Do you go ahead with the hits?"

"No," he said, giving that gentle half-chuckle. "We'll be money ahead. Because the government has screwed up the railroads so well that we're better off now than we would have been if we had wiped out Amtrack three years ago."

"Ten percent," I suggested.

"A million-one? That's steep."

"It's fair," I said.

Slowly, he said, "Yes, I suppose it is. Okay. Go ahead with what you have to do. There won't be any more heat."

Laura's voice was slurred as, in the back seat, she laughed and reassured me, "Not to worry, old friend."

16

Vito Sinatra was probably a whiz at jockeying booze-filled Lincolns during prohibition, but he didn't know anything at all about getting out of an icy ditch.

I showed him how.

"Back up. Not too fast! Then cut your wheels to the right."

"Won't that put my front wheel in the ditch too?"

"Sure. But by then your rear one'll be out, and you'll have traction again. Back the car down the hill as far up the other side as you can, and get a running start. By then, I'll be out of your way."

He thanked me. "I'll be in touch, Warren. But be careful. Out there somewhere are still the ones who hung three of our men in the trees."

"Not to mention somebody who planted Vince Hartman. Okay, I'll try to find your money. But if I so much

181

as get a glimpse of Fred and Charlie—sorry, Chauncey —I'll blow the bastards away. I mean it, Vito."

"Of course," he said calmly.

I watched as he backed down the hill. It took him two tries to get his wheels back up on the rough road, but he made it.

Joan was still huddled in the seat of my rented Toyota.

"It took you long enough," she grumbled.

"It was worth it."

"Did you sell out?"

"Sell out?" I considered the wording. "No, not out. I made a deal to give them something they wanted in exchange for something *I* wanted."

"Hah!"

I had cleverly retained the remnants of Laura Jackson's bottle of Black Velvet. I presented it to Joan.

"Take a swig of that."

She did. Then, raspingly, she repeated, "Hahhh!"

Now was as good a time as any.

I took out the moldy B.P. credit card and handed it to her.

She squinted at it for a moment, showing no reaction. Then she whispered, "I *knew* it!"

"I'm sorry, Joan."

"Where did it happen? When?"

"Up at the Dassow mansion. When? My guess is three years ago. I don't know what happened, but it was fast. He didn't feel a thing."

"How comforting."

"I'll find out who did it."

"Why?"

"Because I'm being paid to."

"Vito?"

"Yes."

"That's stupid! His outfit did it!"

"I don't think so. If they did . . . well—"

She gripped my hand. "You'll lead me to the one who did it."

"Why?"

Her grip became tighter. "You know why."

"You sound like somebody out of a Japanese movie."

"Warren . . . !"

"No. It's not your line of work. I'll take care of the bastards."

She slapped my face. In the cold night, it stung in slow motion. First the impact, then a warm sensation, and eventually a little pain. Not much of a slap, all things considered.

I asked, "Joan, what the hell does it matter who pulls the trigger on them?"

"Because I *want* it. It's a piece missing from me, and I'll never be whole until I find that piece and get it back."

I sighed. "Okay. Your description is a little purple, but I got your meaning. I'll do the best I can."

She sagged down against me. "I know you will, Warren. Hon, I'm cold, and I'm tired."

"I'll take you home."

"No. Take me with you."

Like I said (Or, is it *as* I said? And who cares?), you may not ever know precisely where you are on those back country roads, but you can't get lost either, because you will always end up coming out someplace familiar.

We did. Fifty yards up the road from Lenny's.

Without prompting, Joan said, "Let's."

We charged in like stiff-limbed snow bears, all covered with frozen snow and sleet. I called for hot rum toddies and got, instead, that ubiquitous Adirondack refresher, ginger brandy.

When I reached for my money, Lenny raised his hand. "They're on the house. I owe Miss Hartman for a hundred pounds of venison."

The same teams of pool players were still at it. One looked up and nodded at me. Ben Shaw.

He said something to the other players, put down his cue stick, and came over.

"I hear you were the one who found Harry," he said.

"Guilty."

"I might just take you up on that. It seems to me you've been too goddamned close to the bone during all these hangings. Oh, I heard how you stood off Oscar Deep, but I ain't that easy, Stone."

"Shaw, I'm sorry about your friend Harry. But I didn't put him in that tree. I only found him there."

"That's what you say." His breath was ripe with

cheap bourbon. "And suppose *I* say you bought off the big bad Sheriff? How do you like that?"

Before I could answer, Joan said softly, "Mr. Shaw?"

He turned to her saying, "Yes, ma'am?" and she hit him over the head with a nearby beer bottle.

It shattered, blood burst from his hairline, and he went down to both knees.

Lenny yelled, "Jesus! You two, get the hell out of here before he gets up! He'll kill you."

The pool players started moving toward us. They still had their cue sticks.

I said, "We were just leaving." I dragged the protesting Joan to the door and half-shoved her into the Toyota.

As I spun gravel and ice getting out of the parking lot, I said, "Thanks for protecting me."

"Don't mention it. That loudmouth. Do you know what he tried this morning while we were driving up that mountain?"

"I can guess."

She told me anyway, and it didn't sound all that bad to me, just another case of the old octopus fingers, but I made sympathetic noises.

Let's face it, Stone. With all of the horror going around you, it's hard to be shocked over a drunk playing grabass.

But, come to think of it . . .

Why had Shaw been fired so soon after the big meeting up on the hill?

Joan asked, "Where are we going?"

"Down to my motel. Lean back and relax. It's a good hour away."

"Is there anything there you really need?"

I thought about that. "Toothbrush, soap, that sort of thing."

"What's wrong with that motel up ahead? The Dew Drop Inn. I bet they furnish soap with their rooms. And if you don't know how to scrub your teeth with a washcloth, I'll show you."

It put my back up. "Lady," I said, "I prefer to make my own propositions."

"Fine," she said. "But why not make them here instead of driving another hour?"

It made sense.

I pulled into the driveway of the ramshackle motel, with its broken red neon sign that said, VAC NCY.

I said, "I want you to know that I don't do things like this very often."

As a matter of fact, I didn't this time, either.

The closing door of the motel room was a huge knife blade that cut all the strings holding her up. The CLICK of the lock was still echoing around the fancy imitation wood paneling and the Armstrong plastic floor when she gave a little cry and fell down on the nearest bed.

"Oh, my God!" she whispered. "He's really dead."

It had taken some time, but it had finally hit her. And when it did, it arrived with a roaring vengeance.

I tried to tell her that she had known the truth all along, that this was only confirmation of that, but it was

186

like talking to an eight-track tape. She didn't really say many more words, but she cried and keened, and I felt like the Frankenstein monster trying to reassure the little girl by the side of the river.

Eventually, she quieted down into something that resembled sleep. I showered, and then covered her with the other blanket from my own bed, and slept under the cold sheets until dawn rescued me by shoving icicle fingers into my eyes.

The morning was better.

She had awakened while I lay on my frozen mattress, covered me back up with my donated blanket, gotten herself together in the mildewed john, and then waited patiently until life returned to my frozen body.

Without preamble, when I sat up blinking at the pale sunlight, she said, "You don't think the boys killed him, do you?"

"Huh?"

"If they didn't, who did?"

"Huh?"

"Aren't you awake?"

"I am. I'm awake. Just give me a minute."

I needed more than a minute. She realized this, and said, "I'll go get some coffee."

She left. I curled up under the blanket. The numbness was leaving my toes. Sure, there's a fuel shortage, but what did the management of the Dew Drop Inn think I was, Frosty the Snowman?

Her question worked its way through my head.

There's a failing we people in investigative work have, we always tend to aim the blame toward someone we've met, or at least heard of. There's a good reason for this. We all grew up on a diet of Perry Mason, Agatha Christie and John D. MacDonald. Their rule was to always play fair with the reader, give him all the clues so he had an honest chance to pick out the nasty from the other cast of characters.

In fiction, this is easy. The author decides who did the dirty deed, conceals guilt with a clever series of snowstorms and black smoke, then at the end triumphantly reveals the identity of the killer.

But in real life, we often never meet or even hear of the bad guy until we find ourselves standing face to face in court, or worse, looking over a revolver barrel. Hopefully ours, not his.

So, while we are running around up at the Dassow mansion, or scaling the slopes of the Adirondacks, or freezing in the Dew Drop Inn, some character we never even knew existed may be plotting to hang a few more Mafia soldiers from the nearest tree.

Swell.

Coffee. I could smell its aroma through the door. And I was right. Joan came in with one of those blessed white paper bags with the dark soggy bottoms, and gave me a styrofoam cup filled with steaming, dark black, battery acid.

I poured down a swig, searing my tonsils, and thanked her.

"Is your mind working now?" she asked.

"I hope so."

"I was thinking. What about our buddy, Ben Shaw?"

"What about him?"

"Couldn't he have killed my father?"

"Sure he could have. But why? Where's the gain?"

"Maybe while trying to arrest him?"

"In which case he would have dragged in the corpse, and basked in television glory."

"But if it was murder—?"

"While making an arrest? Come on, kid. Even in Montana, you must have heard of suspects attempting to escape. No, the only way Shaw stacks up is if he had some reason other than legal."

"What about all that money?"

"Sure. But why, then, is he out shooting everything that moves just to fill his freezer? If I had eleven million dollars, I'd be munching on roast beef in Argentina."

"That's how much there was? Eleven million?"

Me and my big mouth. She'd been pumping me, and I had taken the bait.

"In round numbers," I said. "Joan, the way it looks, your father hijacked it. That's why they stripped your mother clean. They thought they were only getting back a little of their own."

"You make them sound like pleasant bankers balancing their books."

"They're anything but pleasant. But they have their code. It saved your life today, so don't knock it."

She tried her own coffee, didn't like it, but decided that it was good for her and drank it anyway. "All right.

189

Well, I've got work to do."

"What about the hanged men?"

"Bodies in trees don't have anything to do with me."

"Not even Harry's?"

"You already know what I thought of Harry. All that concerns me is what happened to my father. If I can help you on the other, I will. But don't ever forget the reason I came here."

"Fair enough. Well, you can help me right now by visiting the john while I get dressed."

"Modest?" she challenged.

"Not a bit. But it's a convention I observe, because if I don't, it might just lead to other things."

"So?"

"No, thanks. I don't sleep with the victims."

"Is that what you see me as?"

"Ask yourself. In the bathroom."

She got up and, balancing her coffee, tried to stalk out of the room. It was a bad stalk. It looked more like a trainee acrobat sliding across the high wire.

Dressing, I called out, "If you mean it, about helping me, I've got a job for you."

"What?"

"Haunting the county land records. I need some hard information about Harry Dassow."

"Okay, I can handle that. Can I come out now?"

"Now." I zipped up.

You may think it funny that I preserve these rather useless vestiges of privacy, but if so, think again. Once somebody has seen you in your skivvies, things are

190

never the same. For better or worse.

"Breakfast?" Joan asked.

"You're on."

I dropped her off at the squat granite building in Old Forge where a phone call had revealed that the real estate records were stored. I drove around the block while she checked to be sure she could consult them. I didn't want my face seen inside. She was in the doorway on my second circuit, and gave me a circled thumb and forefinger. Nice gesture.

As I set off for Bear Paw, the snow was blowing heavily across the road. The wind was out of the northwest. All indications were for a bad storm soon. That's something the high country deer hunters like. It blocks out the city hunters, and puts a patina of danger on the expedition.

I parked outside the Sheriff's office and went in.

He was on the phone. He waved me to a chair. I waited, while he chewed out some deputy about the way a traffic case had been handled.

Laura brought in a cup of coffee and gave it to me.

"You look sleepy," she said. "Were you out late?"

"Up on the mountain. Looking around."

"You be careful," she said. "It's against the law to shine a light when you're armed."

"I'll remember."

Deep hung up. "How about some of that brew for me?"

"Coming up," she said, and left.

"Well," he said. "We heard you'd left town."

"I did. But not for keeps."

"That's too bad."

"How so?"

"The word is, somebody's got it in for you. The word is, all of a sudden the weather around here might turn unhealthy for you."

"You too, Sheriff?"

"Me too what?"

"What you said sounded mighty like a threat."

He waved his hand. "Wrong. Merely advice. Good advice. We've had enough blood around here that we couldn't prevent, if heading off some more by giving you a road map, why that's what I figure to do."

"I've already got a map, Sheriff. And there's a couple of well-marked routes on it."

"Such as?"

"Why did you fire Ben Shaw?"

"Who said I did?"

"He was let go from the department. And there's hard feelings between you."

"Say there are. They might be personal."

I slid my coffee cup across the desk. It slopped over and made a wet track. "Come off it, Deep. Why the hell are you being so coy with me? Anytime the name of the other is mentioned, you both blow up like bulls and paw the turf. Answer this, Sheriff. Was Shaw in on that mob bust-up at the Dassow place?"

"All the way." Just then, Laura came in with his coffee, and he took it. "Thanks." She waited until she was sure he had nothing else to say, then left once more.

"Nice coffee," said the Sheriff.

"Nice," I agreed.

Neither of us was talking about the coffee, and we both knew it.

"What do you mean, Shaw was in it all the way?"

"Somebody made us a blind phone call. Shaw followed it up. Hell, that boy earned himself all kinds of goodies. He could have been my assistant. And once I go, sheriff. That ain't going to be too much longer, either. Once that pension clicks into place, it's bye-bye snow. I like the sunshine action down in Tampa."

"What soured it between you two?"

"Something I've never really understood. He came boiling in here one morning and flat out accused me of cutting him out of some kind of promise I was supposed to have made. But I never made him no promises, none except that after the good work he did up at the mansion, that I'd see he got took care of. And I was making good on that, too."

"How?"

"I had papers in for him. Promotion, a raise. A county car that he could keep at home."

"All the usual perks?"

"Perks?"

I decided against trying to translate the British system of low salaries and high perquisites to make up for the low pay. Instead, I said, "Freebies."

He chuckled. "Like apples on the beat for the flat-foot? Boy, you're sure old-fashioned."

"That I am. Okay, what happened then?"

"Nothing. He practically threatened me, and I told him to go ahead and take his best hold. So he up and quit."

"They say over at Lenny's that you fired him."

"Yeah, that's what they say."

"But if you didn't, why do you let the story spread?"

"Because if I'd fired him, he could collect unemployment. If he'd quit, he couldn't. Now, sixty a week might seem like small potatoes to you, with your twenty-thousand-dollar fees, but to a man like Ben, even though he'd bad-mouthed me, it was something I couldn't take away. Only I don't expect you to understand."

I took a sip of my coffee, feeling the shame tighten my throat. "You're wrong," I said. "I understand."

Back in Old Forge, I circled the squat stone building again, tooting my horn four times on the first pass. On the second, Joan was waiting for me on the sidewalk. She threw open the door and piled in, her hair plastered with new snow.

"Brrr!" she said, making a big thing out of chattering her teeth. "The cold in Montana is better. Dry."

"Did you find anything?"

"You bet. Let's go someplace warm."

"Beer?"

"What time is it?"

"Eleven."

"Beer."

I drove around until I found Joe's place, where Sheriff Deep had introduced me to kielbasi sausages.

Joan reacted well to them, with cries of delicious pain and requests for more. It was half an hour in another place for us, with the events of the past two days blotted out.

But, after two beers, it was time for work again.

"Give," I said. "What did you find?"

"Surprises. Our dear departed friend, Harry Dassow, was flat on his ass, mortgaged up to his eyes. Every acre of land up there on his mountain actually had somebody else's name on it."

"The same name?"

"You said it."

"Whose?"

"Hold onto your seat, my friend."

"Holding."

"Laura Jackson."

I blinked. Tossed down another swig of beer. "Laura?"

"As in mousy lady lawyer."

I managed a sick grin. "I wouldn't know about the mousy part, but—"

"The nice old lady in the records file put me onto her. I had looked through the mortgage section without finding a thing. But there's another way of buying land around here, she informed me. It's called a land contract, and that's how Harry had set it up. All in all, he apparently collected around a quarter of a million dollars, and it was all secured by land contracts he had signed over to your Miss Jackson."

I had already figured out most of it. But not the name on the bottom line. Well. And still driving that beat-up old Chevy with the chocolate smell. Some smart little lady.

"Why?" I wondered.

"Why would she want that land? My little old lady confided in me that there'd be a pile of money in lumbering off that mountain. And two additional piles if the new owner didn't give a damn about the environment. Figure a million-three per pile."

"No. What I meant was, why did Harry Dassow need all that money?"

"And more to the point," Joan said, "where did your mousy Miss Jackson lay her pointed fingers on it?"

"Yes," I agreed. "That's a good question too."

17

Driving up to the ruins of the Dassow mansion again, Joan asked me, "What did you do with my rifle?"

"It's in the trunk."

I had called Sam Keith on the CB, and told him to meet us there. And to bring a shovel. He protested, but not very hard.

This was the crunch. Either I was right, or my whole idea of the case was off beam. Either way, I would know soon enough.

I found a little turnoff below the mansion and pulled into it far enough to be concealed from the road.

Indicating the radio, I said, "Do you know how to operate this thing?"

"Sure."

"I want you to stay here in the car. If you hear shooting, take this car down the hill fast and start yelling for help on Channel Nine."

"Oh, hell," she said. "Not that old route again. Stone, don't you know by now that I'm not running out on you, no matter what?"

"You wouldn't be running out," I said. "You'd be saving my neck. If it comes to shooting, I'm going to be on the run myself, and the faster you get the law up here the better."

"If it's that tight, why don't you get them up here now instead of waiting?"

"I've got to play it this way," I said.

I got out of the car, checked my pistol to be sure she hadn't unloaded it on me last night, and tucked it down inside my pants. "Now you do like I said."

"Yes, boss," she told me.

I didn't really believe her, but she seemed docile enough in the front seat of the Toyota, and I had no choice anyway. So I hiked the rest of the way up to the mansion.

It's not often I get fooled on a stakeout. There were plenty of old ruts in the road, made in the past few days, but they had filled in with snow. I would have bet my life nobody had been up the hill in the past twelve hours.

As it turned out, I was wrong, and I *was* betting my life.

They were waiting behind two big spruce trees. They let me pass, then stepped out behind me.

"Nice and easy," said a voice. I stopped, slipping a little on the snow.

I knew that voice. Chauncey "Charlie" Roberts.

"Hands on your head," said the other voice. "Turn around slow."

I did precisely what they'd instructed. I didn't need to see the high-powered rifle Fred was holding on me to know it was there.

"Vito isn't going to like this," I said.

Chauncey, his pants leg split up to his knee to accommodate the heavy bandage and cast on his leg, said nasty things about Vito. And nastier things about me.

He frisked me and relieved me of my pistol. He tucked it in one of his back pockets.

Fred said, "Vito's been behind a desk too long. We figure that if we get back that eleven million, he'll let us off the hook. It's worth a try. We're sure up the creek now."

"Sorry about that," I said. "But it was your own clever idea to hang Harry Dassow up like a stuck hog."

"Harry had it coming," said Chauncey. "He was playing both ends against the middle."

"How's that?"

"He borrowed a lot of money down in New York. Nobody twisted his arm. Then he started complaining about the vigorish. He knew what it was going to cost him, going in. Anybody else, he'd have had his legs busted to teach the other suckers a lesson. But Harry convinced us he knew where the stash was."

"From the meeting three years ago?"

Fred nodded. "It seemed logical. The meeting was held on his place."

I hoped that Joan had gotten an urge to modulate on the CB airwaves. I said, "There's one big flaw in your conclusions. If Harry had knowledge of where that money was, why did he have to borrow from a shark?"

"Yeah," said Chauncey. "Only we didn't think of that at the time. We grabbed him and tried to get him to tell us where it was. He made a run, he got shot. So we decided to hang him up to warn off those other jokers who were hitting our troops."

"Why did he need all that cash anyway?"

"Some broad had her claws in him."

CLICK! Somehow it was all very poetically right. I had a mental image of two deadly spiders devouring each other, each convinced that the other was the victim.

Down the hill, I heard a car engine. It had the familiar snarl of Sam's jeep.

"I think that's the cavalry," I said. "How did you boys get up here anyway?"

"There's a back road, and we hiked over the hill," said Chauncey.

"Which you discovered while you were tracking Harry?"

He nodded. "I still don't understand Vito getting so hot. Dassow had it coming, and it was sure in hell a boss warning to whoever's been hanging our troops up in the trees."

"Okay, but meanwhile I don't think you guys mean to kill me too, or you'd have done it already."

"No," said Fred. "What we mean to do is wait until your buddy Keith shows up, and then the two of you are going to take us where that money is."

"We don't know where it is."

"Wrong. You may not know, but your buddy sure in hell does."

I started to protest, but then I didn't, because he was probably right.

Sam didn't seem too surprised to see my captors.

"Great," he said accusingly. "Warren, you set me up."

"Not deliberately. These guys think you know where the rest of the eleven million is."

"They're wrong."

"Knock it off," said Fred. "Do you think you two birds are the only ones in the county with a radio? Stone, we heard you tell him to bring a shovel. Why else would you need one, except to dig up the dough?"

"I told you, we don't know anything about your money," I said. "The shovel's to dig up Vince Hartman."

Chauncey stared. "Vince? You found him?"

"The one and only. Why, did you have anything to do with planting him?"

Sam said, "You stupid bastard!"

It took me a second to realize that he was talking to me, not the others.

Another click in my head. If I had been a cartoon

character, a light bulb would have gone on over my head in a little thought balloon.

I tried to shift focus. "Somebody shot Hartman three years ago. I don't suppose you two know anything about that?"

"Hell, no," said Fred. "But what I'd like to know is, if you guys found him, why didn't you call the law? Why are you sneaking around here to dig him up?"

"Stupid!" said Chauncey. "Because the money's buried with him."

"Wrong, but close." I was stalling for time. "It's buried under him, isn't it, Sam?"

My old friend said, "You've got a big mouth."

"Well," said Fred Chapman, "let's stop wasting time. Come on, show us where to dig."

"Then what?"

"All we want's the money," Chauncey lied cheerfully. "We'll flatten your tires and bash your radio so you'll have to walk out of here. That'll give us enough time to split."

Sam glanced at me. In the old days, that would have been the signal for both of us to jump them. But this wasn't the old days. I could probably have taken out Chauncey. But I wasn't going to risk my life on what Sam would do. Not any more.

"I think you'd better show them, Sam," I said. "Hell, it's only money."

"I don't think so," he said.

"What choice do we have?" I asked. I hoped that he

wasn't going to try to make a move by himself.

He wasn't.

Fred's head came off.

It really did. Of all the wounds I've seen, this was the only time I had ever watched a man being decapitated by a shotgun blast.

One moment he was standing there, a hunting rifle in his hands, and the next he was a tottering hulk, headless, spurting blood six feet into the air from his severed jugular. His arms and legs twitched as, slowly, he fell into the snow.

Chauncey leaped back. He waved both hands.

"No, Jesus, no!" he screamed. "Not me! I won't—"

I never learned what he wouldn't. The second blast took him in the chest and blew red and black plaid wool all the way through him and out his back. He lurched heavily into a tree and, almost deliberately, slid down it into a sitting position.

I made a dive for the rifle.

Her voice stopped me.

"Don't try it, Warren!" said Laura Jackson.

She stepped out from behind the spruces. Sam's Remington 12-gauge shotgun was in her hands. Smoke still curled up from its barrel.

Sam had found my .357 in Chauncey's pocket. He put it into his own.

His eyes flicked all around, but they wouldn't meet mine.

"Now what?" I asked.

"Now we dig it up," he said. He looked at Laura.

She nodded. "We've got to."

"They'll follow you anyplace you go," I warned. "Sam, let it stop. It's not too late."

"It's been too late for three years," he said. "Maybe longer than that. You never knew, but it was me who originally went double in Vienna. That poor bastard who got wasted was only a courier."

"But why?"

"Why not? Damn it, Warren, you eventually turned against the Agency. They were exploiting us. They—"

"I turned against the Agency, yes. But not against our country."

"Country?" He laughed. "Whose country? Nixon's? The KKK's? The NAACP's? The American Indian's? We don't have a country. We never did. That was just bull they had us say in school, the pledge of allegiance."

And now they don't even *say* it, I thought sadly. But that had to wait. Chauncey's glazing eyes, watching me from his seated position against the tree, warned me that I might be joining him sooner than I wanted.

"I'm sorry," I said. "Sam, are you going to terminate me?"

He looked away. That was my answer.

Laura, of course, lied. "Why should we? There's plenty for all of us."

Nice lady. She didn't want me to suffer fear. I almost liked her for it.

"That's different," I said. "Money, I can always use."

What I couldn't use was the sudden blast of buckshot she was going to put through me the moment I wasn't shaming her with my stare. That was one advantage of having gone to bed with her. She couldn't just blow me away the way she had Fred and Chauncey.

I kept her eyes fixed on mine. "You killed Vince Hartman, didn't you?"

She nodded. "He was trying to make a deal with Oscar, to get immunity and a new identity."

"In exchange for?"

"The money. Except he lied. He told me that there was only eight million. He wanted to keep the rest for himself and his family out in Montana."

"What did the Sheriff say to that?"

"He never knew. I was the go-between. Me and Harry."

"It was you bleeding Harry that made him go to the Shylocks?"

"He was stupid. He wouldn't cut off this lousy timber. He had something in his head that it was untouchable. From his father. What is it anyway, only trees."

"So you faked Vince out. He thought he was dealing with the Sheriff, but all the time it was only you and Harry Dassow."

"Mostly me. Harry was too busy trying to cover his debts. That's how I got control of the land contracts."

"Didn't he ever ask where you got all that money?"

She laughed. It was an obscene sound in the snow-filled woods. "He was so glad to get up another payment for those people down in the city, he stopped asking if he could come in when he drove me home."

"How did he get in such a hole anyway?"

"Futures on wheat, would you believe? When President Ford sold all that wheat to the Russians, he sold Mr. Harry Dassow's future right down the river."

Sam was getting nervous. He had played this same game before, keeping someone talking while opportunities built gradually. He said, "Come on, Laura. Let's get to work."

"Wait a minute," I said. "Sam, you know the minute I turn my back, she's going to kill me."

"No she isn't!" he protested. He was trying to believe it himself.

"And maybe you, too. The game's over, Sam. She's finished here. She has to go someplace else fast, and she has to become another person. Why should she leave you around to point the finger at her?"

"That's enough!" said Laura.

"She's a fast shifter in broken-field running," I went on. "Her original plan was to launder that money by taking over Harry's lumbering tracts, but now that all this is out in the open, she's ready to take the Syndicate money and run, because that's her only chance."

He knew what I was doing. But what I'd said bothered him, too.

"Not to worry," she told him. "Let's get up to the mansion so we can get out of here."

"Not to worry," I said. "That's what tipped me off, Sam. The way you both used that phrase. You don't talk like another person unless you spend lots of time together. Was some of it in bed, Sam? Is that what you did to Jenny, to top the rest of it off?"

His fingers plucked at the butt of my Magnum. But he didn't take it out of the pocket. I wished he would. Then I might have a chance to jump for it.

"How did you get into this anyway, Sam?" I went on. I didn't dare leave a moment's slack. "How the hell did you get yourself mixed up with this—creature?"

"Shut up," said Laura. "I've listened to enough. Are you going to—"

"Will you really stand there, Sam, and let her blow my guts out?"

"She's not going to hurt you," he said. "Warren, we'll give you half a million. You know how long that'll carry Alice. So let's stop chewing at each other. You're just like me. All you really want is the money."

Softly, I asked, "How did you get involved with her?"

He looked down at the dark blue shadows in the snow. "I don't know," he said. "It just happened. It was fun to be with somebody more exciting than Jenny, and then this Syndicate thing came along, and suddenly I was more involved than I'd planned, and it was too late to get clear. I needed the money, but she doled it out, so I never really found any way to get far enough ahead to break it off."

"Why didn't you just sneak up here and dig it up one night?"

His voice was inaudible. I could only hear the part where he said, ". . . afraid. Afraid of her."

Gently, I asked, "Sam, who hung those three men?"

207

"Me. She held the gun on them, and I . . ."

"Why?"

"To warn the Syndicate to stop snooping around up here. To chase them off. But . . ."

"Yes?"

"It didn't work. In the old days, I would have known that it wouldn't work. But I guess I forgot."

"You forgot a lot of things, Sam," I said. And, as I spoke, I saw that Laura had made up her mind, and that I was going to have to make my move now, or die there on that freezing mountain.

18

I was poised for the leap that would probably be too slow to save my life when I saw movement among the spruces.

Joan Hartman, carrying her .308 rifle, was drawing a bead on Sam Keith.

Damn it, she was aiming at the wrong one! I gave a negative shake of my head, but I couldn't be sure she'd received it, so I said loudly, "Laura, how did you kill Vince Hartman?"

"Why?"

"Because he was the best. It must have taken a lot of doing."

Again, she gave that cold laugh that echoed of death. "He was a man, that's all. We were sitting in my car. I'd realized that there wasn't any way to get that money while he was alive. The poor sucker. He had his hand up my dress all the way. He went happy, thinking he was going to have one last fling in the back seat. When I shot him, his hand grabbed me so hard that I had bruises for a week."

"Damn it!" said Sam. "Let's knock off this crap! Warren, are you with us?"

"I'm with you," I said, nodding toward him. I had seen Joan's rifle come around to point directly at Laura's back. "Now!"

I was already diving for Sam when I heard the "snap" of the firing pin on an empty chamber.

I'd unloaded the .308 back in the motel, and the bullets were still there in the ash tray.

As I hit Sam's knees and he started to fall, Laura swung around and fired into the trees. I heard Joan scream. Then Sam and I were struggling for possession of my pistol.

"Stop it!" shrilled Laura.

"Like hell!" I shouted, still fighting for the pistol. If she was going to shoot me, it would be while I was still fighting.

Instead, she gave me the butt of the shotgun against my skull. I saw a cluster of atom bombs inside my head, and fell down.

Sam jumped away. I blinked my eyes, trying to focus them. I heard him yell, "No, don't!"

I looked up, into the muzzle of the Remington.

Well. It comes to all of us. But the hollow ache in my

stomach spread rapidly down into my legs and my throat tried to choke out words pleading for mercy. I had to bite down hard on my tongue to keep them in.

"Go ahead, bitch," I said instead. "You always wanted to be a man. Here's your chance to kill like one."

"Not Warren!" Sam shouted. "You can't!"

She was going to. There was that final sadness in her eyes, what they call the good-bye look.

Sam's bullet took her too high. As he squeezed off, not really wanting to do it, he must have flinched. The .357 Magnum slug tore a chunk of meat out of her shoulder and her breasts were covered with a cloak of blood, but she stayed alive long enough to turn toward him and pull the trigger of his own Remington.

I didn't see the buckshot take him, but I heard it, and as I rolled to safety behind a spruce, I heard him coughing and puking up his life into the suddenly crimson snow.

Laura was down. Her left foot began to twitch. I stared at it. It was like watching a fallen puppet, with only one string working.

It kicked little mounds in the snow. The rest of her had lost all movement. Only the foot seemed immortal. I felt like running out and choking it into stillness.

"Warren?" called Joan's voice.

"Stay down!" I yelled. "Are you all right?"

"No, but I'll live," she answered. "Can you get away?"

Laura's foot had finally stopped. "I don't know," I said. "Sam?"

His voice was filled with agony. "Here," he said.

"Is it over?"

I waited for a count of twenty before he said, almost in a whisper, "It's over. Come on out."

I did, cautiously. He had pulled himself up against a log, and sat there, his left hand holding in the raw mess that the buckshot had left of his stomach.

"My shot pulled high," he said. "I didn't really want to do it."

"Don't talk," I said. "Let me look at that."

His other hand still held the Magnum. He winced with the strain, but he managed to point it at me.

"No way." He waved the pistol for emphasis. "Forget it, buddy. Leave it lay."

"I'll get on the radio," I said. "Maybe we can get a medic chopper in here—"

"It's too late," he said. "Sam, don't let Jenny know. If there's anything left between us, cover for me. Some way. You can do it. You were always good at that."

"Oh, Christ, Sam. You sound like you're dying. That's only a flesh wo—"

He ripened the air with a few choice curses that echoed the ones I couldn't say. "I bought it, the whole farm. But, Warren, as God is my witness, I never meant to get in so deep. It was just one lousy break after another, and . . ."

"Forget it," I said.

"No. What I did to you—"

"Not to worry," I told him.

But he didn't hear.

Joan's wound was slight; one ball had taken her through the thigh, and she had lost a little blood.

As usual, Sheriff Oscar Deep arrived before the state troopers.

He sniffed unhappily as he looked around.

"This will take some explaining," he said.

It did. But the outcome was that Sam was recognized as the hero who had saved our lives while fighting off the mobsters and their local correspondent, who had turned on them in a battle over the eleven million dollars.

Oscar Deep believed the story about as much as he believed in Santa Claus, but he made no comment.

However, he confiscated the three suitcases filled with moldy bills, turned them over to the tardy troopers who had finally wised up and put chains on their patrol car.

As we drove down the hill, Joan said, "I really tried to kill her. And the damned gun was empty."

"Be glad it was," I said.

"She had it coming."

"And she got it. But don't ever look back and wish it was you that did it."

She brushed her fingers down my leg. "Warren, I don't think I'll ever understand you."

"Don't try," I said.

"You've killed, more than once. But it doesn't affect you."

"If you believe that," I said, "you'll believe in elves."

She settled down against me and the warmth and good smell of her washed over me and began to cleanse away the blood and death of the cold afternoon.

19

Lenny's venison roast was every bit as good a bash as it had been advertised to be, and Joan and I got drunk as skunks on a whole bottle of ginger brandy, and wound up doing a funny kind of waltz on top of the bar while the crazy hunters cheered and threw their glasses against the juke box, which was the nearest thing around to a fireplace. Shadow, the big black dog, ate so many venison steaks that he fell asleep on his back, with all four legs poking straight up into the air. Lenny became maudlin and insisted on reciting "The Face Upon the Floor," and as he reached its climax,

"'Then as he placed another lock upon the shapely head,
With a fearful shriek he leaped and fell across the picture
    —dead!'"

the door to the frozen outdoors opened and in came Ben Shaw, his head bandaged, and a scowl on his face. It sobered me up instantly.

Joan reached for a beer bottle.

He held up both hands. "No," he said. "No more."

I went over and spoke to him quietly. "You were wrong," I said.

"I know it now."

"Deep didn't have anything to do with that money up on the hill. It was all Laura."

"Yeah. I thought he was in on it, and he'd cut me out. I called him up this morning. We're having a beer Sunday. Maybe I'll come back to Bear Paw."

"So everything's all right now?"

"It is with me."

"Good," I said. "With that out of the way, let me tell you that you're a loud-mouthed, greedy slob. Do you want to go outside?"

He had drawn back as I spoke. His eyes locked with mine, wavered, then withdrew.

"You got no call to put your mouth on me like that."

"I've got every right. How about it, Shaw?"

"Aw, you're drunk."

He turned away.

Which of us had won? And what did it matter? Maybe he was right, maybe I had no call to speak to him at all. But my mind was filled with the sight of Sam Keith, bleeding his life away on a mountaintop because he was too proud to let his wife know he had succumbed to the weakness that tempts all of us.

216

I had found a package with ninety hundred-dollar bills in my van that morning, with a note saying, "You did your best. A Sinatra never welshes." The money burned my hands. I thought about Jenny. But that was as far as it went. She would have thrown it in my face. When we brought Sam down the mountain, she was waiting at the hospital, and all she did was stare into my face and see there the failure of my promise not to let anything happen to him.

Lady, it wasn't my fault. I did all I could. Sorry, but he brought it on himself.

She turned away from me.

So who the hell was I to come down on poor Ben Shaw because he didn't share my noble sentiments about honor, and honest hunting of the white-tailed deer, and because he'd tried to play grabass with a girl I liked rather too much?

I looked for him to say I was sorry, but he misunderstood, and cut out.

I think it was Joan who finally drove me back to the motel. But when I woke up, she wasn't there.

In the movies, there's a note, or a forgotten handkerchief; some link to the future.

Not now.

Well, what right did I have to expect anything more?

It was time to go our different ways, bent under our various loads of guilt and failure and attempts to change the inevitable. Me, I went straight to Louisville, Kentucky, to the Polytechnic Hospital where Doc Ewbank gave me his semiannual lecture about the virtues of the state hospital, and curtly refused the envelope with the nine thousand bucks in it.

"Your account's up to date," he said. "Why don't you buy yourself a good drunken weekend?"

I didn't bother to tell him that I'd already had one. Instead, I asked, "Can I stay a while?"

"Why not?"

So I went into the intensive care unit, and sat myself down beside the Bennett MA-1 respirator and listened to it hiss as it pushed air through an incision in her throat. She didn't look like my Alice, and hadn't for more than two years. She weighed less than 80 pounds, and her hair fell over the pillow in waxen strands. Her complexion was sallow, no memory of its rosy glow left at all. She lay on her side, drawn up in a tight fetal position, and tubes were everywhere, penetrating her flesh and her orifices.

There was no thought of touching her. Her mouth, rigid in a corpselike grimace, might never have been kissed. Her hands, once so caressing, were tightly clenched, and if the staff forgot to cut the nails, would draw blood from her palms.

They've told me often that she cannot hear me, but I spoke to her anyway. I told her about the mountains and the snow, and the hot Polish sausage. I even mentioned the ginger brandy.

But I didn't tell her about Sam.

218